The Diamond Bikini

CHARLES WILLIAMS was born in Texas in 1909. His formative years between 1929 and 1939 were spent at sea with the US Merchant Marines as a Radio Operator. Later occupations continued in the radio, shipyards and electronics industries, and he did not turn to writing until the early 1950s.

The influence of the sea was a major one on his crime writing, and many of his novels take place in marine settings or at sea, thus carving an unusual niche for Williams as a highly original, quirky author who was also fascinated by amoral women and protagonists in dead-end and sticky situations.

A strong sense of irony and, sometimes, downright bawdy humour also permeate some of his land-bound novels set in back-country bayou regions of the American South. By combining elements of James Cain and Erskine Caldwell, Williams created a new crime sub-genre.

A prolific author for the paperback original market, Williams averaged a novel a year until 1975 when he committed suicide by drowning off his boat. Five movies have been made from his novels and screenplays.

His novels were *Hill Girl, Big City Girl, River Girl, Hell Hath No Fury, Nothing in her Way, A Touch of Death, Go Home, Stranger, Scorpion Reef, The Big Bite, Girl Out Back, Man on the Run, Talk of the Town, All the Way, Uncle Sagamore and his Girls* (a sequel to *The Diamond Bikini*), *Aground, The Sailcloth Shroud, Nude on Thin Ice, The Long Saturday Night* (filmed by François Truffaut), *Dead Calm, The Wrong Venus, And the Deep Blue Sea* and *Man on a Leash.*

Series Editor: Maxim Jakubowski

blue murder

David Goodis
The Burglar

Davis Grubb
The Night of the Hunter

William P. McGivern
The Big Heat

Charles Williams
The Diamond Bikini

blue murder

THE DIAMOND BIKINI

Charles Williams

SIMON SCHUSTER

First published in 1956
First published as a Blue Murder paperback by
Simon & Schuster Limited 1988

© Charles Williams 1956

Simon & Schuster Limited
West Garden Place, Kendal Street
London W2 2AQ

Simon & Schuster Australia Pty Limited
Sydney

British Library Cataloguing in Publication Data

Williams, Charles, *1909–1975*
    The diamond bikini.
    I. Title
    813'.54[F]   PS3573.I448

    ISBN 0–671–65275–3

Printed and bound in Great Britain by
Richard Clay Ltd, Bungay, Suffolk

The Diamond Bikini

One

Oh, that was a fine summer, all right.

Like Pop says, farms are wholesome, and you just naturally couldn't find a wholesomer one than Uncle Sagamore's. There was a lake where you could catch real fish, and I had a dog, and there was all the rabbit hunters with tommy guns, and Miss Harrington. She was real nice, and she taught me how to swim.

Miss Harrington? Oh, she was the one with the vine there was such a hullaballoo about. You remember. It was in all the papers. It was a tattooed vine, with little blue leaves, winding around her off bosom like a path going up a hill, and it had a pink rose right in the centre. Pop raised hell with me because I didn't tell him about it sooner but, heck, how did I know everybody didn't have one? I just sort of took it for granted the Welfare ladies had vines on theirs too, but I never did ask one because when I was with them I hadn't seen Miss Harrington yet, or her vine.

But that's all getting ahead of the story. I better start at the beginning and tell you how we happened to go to Uncle Sagamore's in the first place. It was on account of Pop getting drafted so much.

I guess it was just a bad year for being drafted. The first time Pop got drafted was at Gulfstream Park, along in the winter, and then it was Pimlico, but Aqueduct was the worst of all. We'd hardly got a place to park the trailer and started printing when they drafted him again. And of course the Welfare ladies grabbed me, the way they always do.

Those Welfare ladies are funny. I don't know why, but no matter where they are they're always the same. They ask you the same old questions, and they usually have big bosoms, and when you try to explain how you sort of travel around to all the big cities like Hialeah and Belmont Park, and how Pop is a turf investment counsellor, and about him having so much trouble with the draft board, they look at each other and shake their heads and say, 'Oh, how terrible! And he's just a *child*.'

Well, these Welfare ladies at Aqueduct asked me where I go to school, why Mama went away and left Pop, and can I read and write, and so on. And when I told 'em, sure I could read fine they brought in this book to try me out. And, say, that was really a swell book too, what I could dig out of it in the month I was with the Welfare. It was all about a kid named Jim Hawkins and a pirate with one leg named Long John Silver, and it was fun. I sure wish I could get hold of it again so I could find out how they ended up. Do you think there might be another copy of it around?

But to get back to the Welfare ladies, they just looked at each other when they saw how much trouble I was having with it, and said, 'Uh-huh, I thought so.'

And I *was* having trouble with it, sort of. It wasn't that there was any real tough words in it, but the man that put it together had a funny way of writing, spelling everything out the long way.

'Billy, you shouldn't have told us you can read,' the boss lady said. You can always tell which one is the boss, because it's odds-on she'll have a bigger bosom than the others. 'Didn't your father ever teach you that little boys should always tell the truth?'

'But, ma'am,' I says. 'I *can* read. It's just that this stuff is wrote so funny. There's too many letters in all the words.'

'That's ridiculous,' she says. 'How could there be too many letters in the words? Are you suggesting that Robert Louis Stevenson didn't know how to spell?'

'I don't know anything about this guy Stevenson,' I says, 'but I'm just trying to tell you this stuff is wrote funny and nobody could make it out. Look, I'll show you what I mean.'

I still had my baloney sandwich in my pocket because we'd just got to the track when the Pinkertons drafted Pop and I remembered it was wrapped in a sheet of yesterday's racing form. I hauled it out and took a bite of the baloney while I showed 'em.

'Now, here,' I says, pointing to it with my finger. 'Look at this. *Barnyard Gate (M) 105* ch.g.3, by Barnaby – Gates Ajar, by Frangi-Pangi. Dec. 5, TrP, 6f, 1 :13 sy, 17, 111* 1^1, 1^5 1^3, 8,^{9} Str'gf'l'wG AlwM, Wo'b'g'n 119, C'r'l'ss H's'y 112, Tr'c'le M'ff'n 114.* You see? And now take a look at this workout. *Fly 2 Aqu $\frac{1}{2}$ft : 48 3/5 bg.* A morning-glory and a dog, and if you ever put ten cents on his nose even in a two thousand claimer you got rocks in your head. He's a front runner and a choker and even Arcaro couldn't rate him off the pace and he always dies at the eighth pole.'

They stopped me then, and there was hell to pay. They just wouldn't believe I was reading it. I told 'em it was all right there, as plain as the nose on their face, that Barnyard Gate was a three-year-old chestnut gelding and had never won a race, and that he was by Barnaby out of Gates Ajar, by Frangi-Pangi, and that the last time he'd run he'd gone off at about 17-to-1 in a six-furlong Maiden Allowance at Tropical Park on December 5th with George Stringfellow up and carrying 111 pounds with the apprentice allowance claimed. The track was sloppy and the winner's time was 1 minute and 13 seconds, and Barnyard Gate led at the start, at the half, and going into the stretch, and then had folded and come in eighth by nine lengths, and that the first three horses had been Woebegone, Careless Hussy, and Treacle Muffin. I told 'em they was the ones didn't know how to read, and they said, 'Well, I *never*!'

That did it. They said a boy that the only thing he could read was the racing form was a disgrace to the American way of life and they was going to court and have me taken away from Pop and put in a Home. I didn't like it, of course, but there wasn't anything I could do about it and I just had to wait for Pop to get out of the draft.

Well, they kept me at the Home for about a month, and they was real nice to me. They even let me have the Treasure Island book to read, and I got so worked up about it I couldn't lay it down. It was slow going at first, what with this guy's long-winded way of padding the words out, but after a while I worked out a kind of system that I'd squint my eyes and sort of weed out all the extra letters and I did a little better. I was half-way through it and getting more excited all the time when Pop came back from the draft. There was a sort of meeting, with some of the Welfare ladies and the superintendent of the Home and some strange men I didn't know, and they was all going at it hot and heavy, with Pop telling 'em how he was a turf investment counsellor by trade and there wasn't anything wrong with that, and who did they think they was, trying to take his boy away from him?

I was trying to sneak a few lines of the book, just in case they took it away from me, and I says to Pop, 'Do you know about this Long John Silver?'

'I never heard of him,' he says. 'Probably some dog running in claimers.'

Well, they jumped all over him then, and that's when he remembered about Uncle Sagamore's farm. We was going down there, he said; there wasn't nothing like wholesome farm life for a boy. And there's one thing about Pop, he's a talker. When he's selling the sheets he can talk the ear off a sucker. Clients, Pop calls 'em. I could see him beginning to get hold of this idea about Uncle Sagamore's farm, and he really started to warm up.

'Why,' he says, 'just think of all our great men that got their start on a farm, men like Lincoln and General Thomas E. Lee and Grover Whalen and William Wadsworth Hawthorne and Eddie Arcaro. Why, just think what it'll be like, with ducks to feed and eggs to gather, and watermelons, and cows to milk, and horses to ride—' Pop stopped there and kind of coughed a little and backed up.

'No. Come to think of it, there ain't a horse on the place. I remember now my brother Sagamore always said he wouldn't have one around if you give it to him. He's got mules galore, but no horses. He hates horses. Gentlemen, can you think of a more downright wholesome place for a growing boy than a farm like that?' Pop began to get tears in his eyes, just thinking how wholesome it was going to be.

Well, the way it turned out there was a lot more palaver but they finally agreed with Pop about the farm and said I could go. But they warned him if he ever got in any more trouble around New York they'd take me away for keeps. I thought this was kind of funny, because we'd never been in New York, but I didn't say anything.

We went back and got the car and trailer and started out, but we got mixed up in traffic and so turned around we didn't know where we was. Aqueduct is a lot bigger than Hialeah or Pimlico and it's got so many streets you could drive around in it until you starved to death and never find your way out. Pretty soon we was stalled in a traffic jam on a street that had a lot of big hotels with carpets and coloured canvas tents running out the front doors and across the sidewalk, and Pop yelled at a man standing under one of these tents. The man was dressed up in a fancy uniform with a lot of red and gold on it.

'What street is this?' Pop asks.

'Park Avenue,' the man says, kind of snooty.

'Well,' Pop asks him, 'how do you get over to Jersey?'

The man just stared at him and said, 'Who'd want to?' and then went on looking at his fingernails.

'That's the trouble with this goddam place,' Pop says to me. 'What do you want to go anywhere for? You're already here.'

Just then another man in a uniform with a monkey's hat on his head come out the door leading a dog on a leather strap. It was the longest dog I ever saw in my life, with real short legs, and his belly dragged when he come down the steps. The man with the red and gold uniform puffed up and got red in the face, but he took the leather strap anyway, and started down the street with the dog. But just then the dog give a big leap and jerked the strap out of his hand and ran out in the street in the middle of all the cars.

The uniform man followed him, squeezing his way through the cars and getting redder in the face all the time. 'Here, nice doggie,' he says. 'Here, Sig Freed. Nice Sig Freed. I'll kick your teeth in, you dumb sausage bastard.'

But Sig Freed turned and ran down the middle of the street towards us and the next thing I knew he was under our car. The traffic was beginning to move a little now and the people behind us was blowing their horns and calling Pop a knucklehead, and I was afraid Pop would start up with him under there, so I jumped out and crawled in after him. He grinned at me, and yawned, and licked me on the face. I gathered him up and got back in the car with him sitting on my lap, still laughing that cute dog laugh of his.

The uniform man come running up, dodging the cars, and his face was as red as his coat. 'Gimme that damn mutt,' he says, looking hard at Pop.

'Beat it, you poodle-dog walker,' Pop says, 'before I spit in your eye.'

'Give him here! I'll call a cop.'

The traffic was clear up ahead now. Pop held up a finger and says, 'That for you, Mac,' and we started off with a whoosh and just made the next traffic light before it turned red. We turned a corner pretty soon and the man never did catch up with us.

Sig Freed was tickled pink. He licked me on the ear and barked a couple of times, and then stuck his head out the window to grin at all the people along the sidewalk. 'Can I keep him, Pop?' I says. 'Can I?'

'How you going to feed him?' Pop says. 'A dog like that, from Park Avenue, he don't like nothing but mink and caviar.'

'I'll bet he'll eat regular bones, just like any dog.'

'I don't know,' Pop says, 'but how you going to keep him when we get to Hollywood Park?'

'Hollywood Park?' I says. 'Ain't we going to Uncle Saga-more's?'

He shook his head. 'Of course not. I just said that to them nosy old hens.'

That made me feel kind of sad, because I was all pepped up about living on the farm, but I didn't say anything. There ain't no use arguing with Pop. After a while we found a tunnel going under the river and when we come out Pop said we was in Jersey. I didn't say any more about Sig Freed, hoping he would forget he was there and not make me put him out, but every once in a while he would jump up and lick Pop on the face.

'Wet cuss, ain't he?' Pop says, just barely missing a big truck.

But he didn't say anything about making me put him out, and I could see he had something on his mind. He looked kind of worried, and he kept mumbling to hisself. After a while he pulled off the road and counted how much money we had.

'Is it very far from Aqueduct to Hollywood Park?' I asks him.

'It's quite a piece. Take us a week, anyway.'

That night we found a place to camp by a little creek and while he was frying the baloney I asks him, 'Pop, why can't we go to Uncle Sagamore's?'

'Well, for one thing, he may not be there. The last I heard he was about to be drafted.'

'Is he in the printing business too?'

'No,' Pop says. He opened a bottle of beer and sat down on a rock with his sandwich. 'You might say he's more in the manufacturing business.'

'Oh.' I give Sig Freed a piece of baloney. He flipped his head and throwed it, and then pounced on it like it was a mouse and gobbled it down.

'See, Pop,' I says, 'he eats baloney.'

'Well, that's nice of him,' Pop grunts. 'Democratic, ain't he?'

'Can we keep him, Pop?'

'We'll see,' he says. 'But don't bother me now. I got a problem.' He was looking worried again.

Sig Freed went over and started licking the frying pan. He liked the grease. It was dark now, and the fire was pretty under the trees. I got my blankets out of the trailer and unrolled 'em, and laid down with Sig Freed curled up beside me. I wanted to keep him awful bad. Pop opened another bottle of beer.

'Have we ever been to Hollywood Park?' I asks. We been to so many cities I kind of lose track sometimes.

Pop shook his head.

'Why not?'

'Because you got to go across Texas to get there.'

'What's Texas, Pop?' I asks.

'What's Texas? Well, I'll tell you.' He lit a cigar and stretched his legs out. 'Texas is the biggest area without horse racing in the whole world, outside of the Pacific Ocean. I been wanting to go to Hollywood Park and Santa Anita for years, but I ain't never had enough money to get all the way across Texas at one jump, and that's the only way you can get across. One time, before you was born, I started out from Oaklawn Park. I got as far as Texarkana, and headed out into Texas real early in the morning before I could lose my nerve. But the more I thought about it the scareder I got, and in about fifty miles I got chicken and turned back. I ain't never tried it since.'

He looked at the fire and let out a long breath, kind of shaking his head. 'Maybe I'm getting a little old to try it now. A man's either got to be young and full of sass and vinegar and ready to tackle anything, or else he's got to have a lot of money. Texas ain't no place to fool around with. There ain't a race track in a thousand miles in any direction. A man was to run out of gas in the middle of it, he might have to go to work, or something like that. It just ain't safe.'

I could see it had him worried considerable. Every night when we'd camp he'd get out the road maps and measure off with little sticks and count the money we had left, and it always come out the same. We'd run out of gas at a place called Pyote, Texas, halfway between Fairgrounds and Hollywood Park.

'It ain't no use, dammit,' he says the last night. 'We just can't make her. We're going to wind up spank in the middle of Texas, sure as you're born. The only thing to do is hole up at Sagamore's till Fairgrounds opens next fall.'

I let out a yip and hugged Sig Freed and he give me his play growl and licked my ear. And that's how we come to go to Uncle Sagamore's.

Two

It had been a long time since Pop had been to the farm, so after we turned off the paved road he had to stop and ask a man how to get there. There was a little house without any paint on it and a barn made out of logs on the other side of the road. The man was chasing a hog, and he stopped and took off his hat and mopped his face with a red handkerchief.

'Sagamore Noonan?' he says, looking at us kind of funny.

'Yeah,' Pop says.

'You mean you want to go to Sagamore Noonan's?' He couldn't seem to believe it.

'Is there anything wrong with that?' Pop asks, kind of mad. 'He's there, ain't he?'

'Why I reckon so,' the man says. 'Leastwise, I ain't seen 'em bringing him out lately.'

'Well, how do we get there?'

'Well, you just sorta follow this road. The gravel kind of peters out after a while and it's mostly sand, but I reckon you can make her all right with that trailer. After you go over a long sandhill and start down in the bottom there's a pair of ruts leading off to the left through a war gate. From there it ain't over a quarter-mile, and you can smell it if'n the wind's right.' He mopped his face again. 'And if you meet any cars coming out, give 'em plenty of room because they'll likely be in a hurry.'

'In a hurry?' Pop says.

'Yeah. Sometimes the shurf's mighty aggravated when he goes by here. Run over three of my shoats already this year.'

'Well, that's too bad,' Pop says.

The man kind of shook his head, like it was getting the best of him. 'That's the reason I'm chasing this hawg. Two of the shurf's men is back in there now and I'm trying to get him penned up before they come out. Sure is hard on hawgs.'

Pop thanked him and we went on.

'What did he mean, you could smell it?' I asked.

He shook his head, kind of absent-minded, like he was thinking. 'With Sagamore, there ain't no telling.'

We went up over a long hill where there was lots of pine trees. The car began to get hot, pulling the trailer in the sand. After we ran along the top of it for a while and started down on the other side we went around a turn in the road and right up alongside another car pulled off in a little open place where there wasn't any trees and you could see out over the river bottom. A man in a white hat was sitting on top of the car with his feet on the hood and he was looking through a pair of field-glasses like you watch races with. Pop put on the brakes and stopped, and the man let his field-glasses dangle on a strap around his neck and stared at us. I tried to see what he was looking at, but all there was was a couple of fields and then trees as far as you could see.

'What you looking for?' Pop asks.

There was another man inside the car, and he was wearing a white hat too. He got out and they looked at each other.

'Airplanes,' the man on top of the car says.

'Sure enough?' says Pop.

'That's right. We're airplane spotters,' the other man tells him. He had a gold tooth that showed when he grinned. 'Never know when them Rooshians might take a notion to fly over this way. Where you fellas headed?'

Pop stared at him for a minute. 'To the airport,' he says, and started the car up. 'I see any Russian planes, I'll let you know.'

We found the ruts going off to the left, and went through the wire gate. It was downhill a little way through the trees and then all of a sudden we saw Uncle Sagamore's farm.

Then we smelled it.

Pop slammed on the brakes, and the motor stalled. 'Good God,' he says, 'what's that?'

Sig Freed began to whine and jump around in the back seat. Pop took off his hat and fanned the air in front of his face, kind of choking a little. Then in a minute it wasn't so bad and we could breathe again. There had been a little breeze blowing from where the house was, and it had quit.

'It's coming from over there,' Pop says. 'Right there at the house.'

'What do you suppose is dead?' I asked.

Pop shook his head. 'Ain't nothing could ever get that dead.'

We looked around at the farm. At first we didn't see anybody. There was a log barn off to the right, and straight ahead in the shade of a big tree was the house. It was kind of grey, like old wood, and didn't have any paint on it anywhere. There was a big porch across the front. White smoke was coming out of the stove-pipe on the far side of the roof, but we didn't see Uncle Sagamore anywhere.

Then we heard a hammering sound, and looked off to the left. It was downhill that way, and at the bottom of the hill we could see a lake that went off into the trees. And about half-way down the hill a man was working on something. It was the funniest-looking thing I ever saw. I couldn't tell what it was.

'Is that Uncle Sagamore?' I asked Pop.

'Working like that? In the sun?' Pop shook his head and stared at the man and the thing he was nailing boards on. It was about fifty yards away and you couldn't see what the man looked like except he was kind of shiny on top like he didn't have much hair.

'That's not Sagamore,' Pop says. 'But maybe he knows where he is.'

The breeze was still stopped and we didn't get any more of that awful smell, so Pop started the car again and we eased down the hill. I kept watching this thing the man was working on, trying to figure out what it was, but I didn't make any sense out of it. It looked a little like he'd started out to build a boat but changed his mind and wanted to make a house out of it, and then somewhere along the line he'd decided, aw, the hell with it, he'd just go ahead and nail her together and see what it was after he got through.

The bottom part of it was a big box about the size of a small house trailer, and on top of that was another box. None of it was finished yet, and you could see all the way through it in places. A lot of the boards had big holes in them. Some of the holes was round and some was shaped like a new moon. The man was standing on a scaffold about as high as the top of the car, with his back to us, nailing a short board over the hole in another board.

He didn't seem to hear us. Pop stopped the car right in back of him and leaned out the window. 'Hey,' he says, 'where's Sagamore?'

The man didn't even look around.

'Hey, you, up there!' Pop yells.

The man just went on hammering. Pop and I looked at each other. We got out of the car, and Sig Freed jumped out and started running around, stopping now and then to look up at the man and bark.

Pop reached in and honked the horn. The man didn't pay any mind. In a minute he stopped hammering and leaned back a little to look at the board. He shook his head and started pulling it loose with his claw hammer. He moved it over a couple of inches and nailed it down again.

Pop went *wonk! wonk! wonk!* on the horn. The man looked at his board again, but he didn't like it there either and started pulling it loose once more. The board was getting chewed up by now.

'We ain't getting anywhere here,' Pop says, rubbing his hand across his face. 'We want to talk to him, I guess we got to go up there.'

Pop climbed up the ladder and got on the scaffold. I went up behind him. We could see the man from the side here, which was a little better than not seeing anything but his back. He was older than Pop, and he didn't have any shoes on. He was wearing overalls and a white shirt with the sleeves cut off, and he had on a high stiff collar and a tie. The tie stuck down inside the bib of his overalls. There was a little ring of white hair around his head just above his ears, and when he turned towards us his eyes made you think of a man yelling at cars in a traffic jam. Sort of wild-like. Only he didn't act like he saw us.

'It's too late,' he says, kind of shouting and waving the hammer in Pop's face.

'Too late for what?' Pop asks. He backed up and bumped into me.

'No use coming around now. I tried to tell you. All of you. But nobody'd listen. Everybody chasing the almighty dollar and drinking and lying and fornicating back and forth, and now it's too late.'

'Where's Sagamore?' Pop says, yelling in his ear.

'Whole world's busting with sin and corruption. It's a-coming. I tried to tell you. Armageddon's a-coming.'

'Pop,' I says, 'what's Armaggedon?'

'I don't know,' Pop says. 'But he sure as hell ain't going to hear it when it gets here, unless it runs over him.'

Then Pop leaned over and put his mouth right against the man's ear and yelled, 'I'm looking for Sagamore Noonan. I'm his brother Sam.'

'It's too late,' the man says, waving the hammer in Pop's face again. 'I ain't going to take none of you sinners. You can all just drowned.'

Pop sighed and looked around at me. 'I think I know who the old skinhead is now. It's your Aunt Bessie's brother Finley. Used to be a sort of jackleg preacher. Deaf as a post. He ain't heard hisself in twenty years.'

'What do you suppose he's building?' I asked.

Pop shook his head. 'No telling. From the looks of it, he must of forgot, hisself.'

He climbed down the ladder and I jumped down after him. Just then we got another whiff of the smell coming from up at the house.

'You suppose something is dead up there?' I asked.

Pop looked up towards the house, and I looked. We didn't see any sign of anybody. 'Maybe it's one of his mules,' he says.

The man up on the scaffold was still hammering away and muttering to hisself when we got in the car and drove back up the hill. Pop eased up real careful and stopped the car and trailer under the big tree in front of the house while we got ready to hold our noses. But when we got out it seemed like there was a little breath of air blowing up from the lake behind us, and we didn't smell anything. Not at first.

It was real quiet. It was so still you could hear your breath going in and out. I liked it fine, because it was so different from all the noise around big cities like Aqueduct. I looked around. The front yard was bare dirt, beat down flat and smooth, and there was a walk marked off with square brown bottles set in the ground. The front door in the middle of the porch was open, but we didn't see anybody inside. There was still a little smoke coming out of the stovepipe, but not as much as there had been at first.

'Hello!' Pop called out. 'Hello, Sagamore!'

Nobody answered.

'Why don't we just go in?' I asked.

Pop shook his head. 'No. We might surprise him.'

'Ain't it all right to surprise people?'

'Maybe some people,' Pop says. 'But not Sagamore.'

'Well,' I says, 'I don't think there's anybody here.'

Pop looked around, real puzzled. 'Well, you'd think Bessie would be, anyway – Oh, sweet Jesus!' He grabbed his nose and started fanning the air with his hat.

I begin to choke too. 'Pop,' I says, 'it's coming from over there. You see all them tubs, over there by the well?'

He waved an arm. 'See if you can get close enough to find out what's in 'em.'

After you'd had a whiff or two you got a little used to it and you could breathe without choking, so I walked over towards the well. It was off beyond the end of the porch. There was a clothes line strung up between two posts, and the tubs was sitting in the sun just this side of it. There was six of 'em, washtubs, strung out in a row along the side of the house. When I got up close I had to hold my nose again.

There was something in 'em, all right. I couldn't make it out at first. It looked like sort of brownish water with some scum and old thick bubbles floating on top. Then I saw there was something underneath the surface. I got a stick and poked around inside until I could fish part of it up. It was a cowhide. The hair was slipping off it. When I dropped it back, the whole mess bubbled.

It was awful.

I looked at the other washtubs and they was all the same. I yelled and told Pop. He come over, still waving his hat in front of his face. Sig Freed had run under the house and was whimpering.

Pop took a look when I fished one up again, and nodded his head. 'Just tanning some cowhides,' he says, like he wasn't too surprised.

'Is Uncle Sagamore in the tannery business?' I asked.

Pop looked like he was thinking about something. 'What's that? Oh. Not that I ever heard of. Maybe it's sort of a sideline.'

'But what's he got 'em up against the house for? I'd think he'd put 'em about two miles away.'

'Well, I don't know,' Pop says. 'Maybe he's just trying to aggravate Bessie, or something. Anyway, I wouldn't ask him about it, if I was you. Sagamore's sort of peculiar about people asking questions. So when we find him, just kind of ignore the whole thing.'

I started to ask him how you was going to ignore anything as powerful as them tubs, but then I didn't. When it comes to answering a lot of questions, Pop never figures to be laying up close to the pace hisself. Maybe it runs in the family.

I went on around the house, looking for Uncle Sagamore. The sun was straight overhead now, and it was hot. I could hear some kind of bug yakking it up in the trees. I was walking along the bare ground at the back of the house when I thought I heard somebody moving inside. I stopped and listened, but didn't hear it any more, only that bug buzzing away down the hill.

The kitchen door was open. I walked up on the step, which was a block cut out of a big log, and looked inside. I didn't see anybody, so I went on in. Sig Freed jumped up on the block and come in after me. There was a cookstove in one corner, and a table with oilcloth on it, and some chairs.

I noticed a pot sitting on the stove, and went over and lifted the lid, thinking there might be something to eat in it. There was. They was white, and looked like boiled potatoes. I got a spoon off the table and dug a piece out of one. It wasn't a potato, though. It tasted more like a rutabaga. And it was stone cold. It wasn't very good.

There was a door on the left side of the kitchen, and one straight ahead, going into the front. I looked in the room on the left. There was a bed in it, but it was kind of a storeroom. Some sacks of sugar was sitting on the floor, and there was a lot of old harness and clothes hanging along the walls. I came out and started to go into the room in front of the kitchen, when I stopped, remembering something that was funny. It was that white rutabaga. It was cold. But the pot was on a stove with a fire in it.

I went back and looked in the pot again. Then I felt the top of the stove. It was cold too. But I'd seen smoke coming out of the pipe. I stepped back out in the yard and looked up. By golly, there wasn't any smoke now. But there had been. I was sure of that.

I went back in the kitchen, still trying to figure it out, and raised one of the stove lids and put my hand down on the ashes in the firebox. They was as cold as the rutabaga. There sure was some funny things happened around Uncle Sagamore's, I thought.

I could hear Pop yelling hello again, and then calling me, so I went into the front room. It was the living-room. There was a big mud fireplace on the right, with a shotgun lying on some forked sticks up above the mantel. Most of the chairs had bottoms wove out of strips of cowhide with the hair still on. Besides the door that went out on the front porch there was another one on the left that went into another bedroom. I looked in there before I went out. There was nobody in it. The whole house was empty.

When I stepped out on the porch the smell hit me again. It seemed to be worse there than anywhere else. I ran down the steps and out by the car. Pop was there, still fanning the air with his hat and cussing bitter and disgusted like.

'Why in hell didn't I have sense enough to go to Narragansett Park?' he says.

'Aw, Pop,' I says. 'I like it here. Except for the smell.'

'Yeah, but what are we going to do? Sagamore ain't here. He's probably been drafted. Nobody around except that old squirrel down there hammering boards together. Nowhere else around here we can go.'

Right behind us somebody said, 'Howdy, Sam.'

We whirled around, and there was a man standing in the front door, leaning against the jamb with a shotgun hanging in the crook of his arm. I just stared at him. I couldn't figure out how he'd got there. The house had been empty less than a minute ago. And we hadn't heard a sound.

He was a big man, taller than Pop, and he was dressed in overalls and an overall jumper without any shirt. He had kind of small, coal-black eyes and a big hooked nose like an eagle, and his face was covered right up to his eyes with sweaty black whiskers about a quarter of an inch long. His hair was black and grey mixed, growing kind of wild and bushy over his ears, but he had a big bald spot that went from his forehead right across the top of his head. The black hair on his chest showed up past the bib of his overalls and stuck out along his neck where the jumper was open.

Those hard, shiny, button eyes seemed to be kind of grinning while they looked at us, but they made you think of a wolf's grin. There was a big lump in his left cheek, and then without moving his head or anything he puckered up his lips and a big stream of brown tobacco juice sailed out across the porch, kind of bunched up and solid like a bullet. It came on and cleared the front steps and landed *ka-splott* in the yard.

'Visitin'?' he asked.

'Sagamore!' Pop says. 'You old son of a gun.'

So that was Uncle Sagamore, I thought. But I still couldn't figure out where he had come from, or how he'd got there in the door without us hearing him.

He put the gun down against the wall and said, 'Ain't seen you in quite a spell, Sam.'

'About eighteen years, I reckon,' Pop says. We went up on the porch and they shook hands and we all hunkered down on our heels around the door.

'Where did you come from, Uncle Sagamore?' I asked. 'I was just there in the house and I didn't see you. And what's the man building down there by the lake? And how come you didn't put those cowhides further away from the house?'

He turned his head and looked at me, and then at Pop. 'This yore boy, Sam?'

'Yeah, that's Billy,' Pop says.

Uncle Sagamore nodded. 'Going to be a smart man when he grows up. He asks a lot of questions. He'll probably wind up knowing more than a justice of the peace if anybody ever answers any of 'em.'

Uncle Sagamore got up and went in the house. When he come back he had two glass jars with him, and they was full of some kind of clear stuff like water. He set one down just inside the door and handed the other one to Pop, and then hunkered down again. Pop was still fanning the air with his hat, but he didn't say anything about the smell from the tubs.

He took a drink out of the jar and then handed it back to Uncle Sagamore. He gasped a little, and tears come to his eyes.

'Old well ain't changed a bit,' he says.

They didn't fool me any, of course. I knew it wasn't water but I didn't say anything.

Uncle Sagamore took the big wad of tobacco out of his cheek and threw it out in the yard. He tilted the jar up and his Adam's apple went up and down. He wiped his mouth with the back of his hand. It didn't make any tears in his eyes, though.

'By the way,' Pop says, 'there was a couple of airplane spotters up on the hill as we come in. Looking down this way with field glasses.'

'Wearin' white hats?' Uncle Sagamore asked.

'Yeah,' Pop says. 'And one of 'em had a gold tooth. Looked like fellers that was real pleased with theirselves.'

Uncle Sagamore nodded, sort of solemn. 'That was some of the shurf's men. Real hard-workin' fellers, always frettin' about forest fars. They spend a lot of time up there watching for smoke.'

'They ever find any?' Pop asked.

'Well, sometimes,' Uncle Sagamore says. 'Once in a while an old stump will catch afar from lightnin' or something down there in my bottom timber. By God, they never miss her, neither. They come oozin' out of the bushes from every direction like young'uns to a fish fry.'

He took another drink out of the jar, and kind of chuckled. 'Other day there was an old rotten log a-burnin' down there, and you know some careless idiot must of left twenty, thirty sticks of dynamite lyin' around pretty close to it. Probably been shootin' stumps, or something. Anyway, just about the time all these courthouse far-eaters come a-chargin' in through the bushes she started lettin' go. Damned if them fellers didn't just about clear off a whole acre of new ground for me, gettin' out of there. Never seen men could tear down so much brush tryin' to get their feet headed in the same direction.'

Pop took another drink out of the jar. 'Sure gives a man a comfortable feeling,' he says, 'to know his law officers is on the job like that, looking after things.'

'That's right,' Uncle Sagamore says. 'Matter of fact, they'll be down here any minute now.'

Just then there was a loud racket up the hill where the wire gate was. It sounded like a car had run through the gate without bothering to open it first. Then we saw the car. It was plunging and bouncing down the hill like Nashua running over cheap horses in the stretch. There was a big cloud of dust boiling up behind it, and every once in a while it would hit a bump and go three feet in the air. They sure was in a hurry.

'Been meaning' to take a fresno and smooth that road down a mite for them boys,' Uncle Sagamore says, watching them buck down the hill. 'Sure is hell on us taxpayers, the way they tear up County cars gettin' in and out of here.' He stopped and shook his head. 'Just never seem to get around to it, though, with all there is to do.'

While he was talking he reached the jar back in through the door and traded it for the one that was inside. 'Guess the boys might want a little dram with us,' he says. He handed the new jar to Pop, just like he had the other one.

'I'd be careful about lettin' any of her go down,' he says. 'She might have a little croton oil in her.'

'Oh,' Pop says. He tilted his head back and took a swig, but he didn't seem to swallow. I asked them what croton oil was, but when they didn't say anything I remembered Uncle Sagamore didn't like to answer questions.

Just then the car put on its brakes and the tyres screamed. It slid about thirty feet and come to a stop under the tree. Uncle Sagamore looked up like he'd just now noticed it for the first time, took the jar away from Pop, and put it down on the floor to one side of him where it was out of sight from in front. The two men that had been looking for aeroplanes got out and started towards us. The smell hit 'em, and they started to sputter and choke and wave the air with their hats, but they kept coming, kind of grinning at each other.

Uncle Sagamore reached out a hand and moved the shotgun a little, like he didn't think it had been standing just right before. 'Come on up and set, boys,' he says.

They come on up the steps. The gold-tooth one was tall and skinny and had a nose nearly as big as Uncle Sagamore's, and a long jaw, like a horse. His hair was kind of a buttery colour, clipped off close along the sides of his head and real long on top and slicked down with hair oil. The other one was skinny too, but he wasn't as tall. He had dark wavy hair and one of them fancy moustaches that look like they'd been painted on your upper lip with a fountain pen. His sideburns come way down on his jaw.

They both had wise grins on their faces.

They fanned the air with their hats, and the gold-tooth one says, 'Sorry we broke down your gate, but we was in a hurry to get here before you could drink any more of that well water. Wanted to warn you there's been a lot of typhoid going around.'

'Well sir, is that a fact?' Uncle Sagamore says.

They looked at each other again like they was going to bust out laughing, in spite of the awful smell. 'Sure is,' the moustache one says. 'And you know, the shurf told us just this morning, he says you boys be sure to bring in a sample of water from Sagamore Noonan's well so we can have it analyzed. Sure as hell wouldn't want Sagamore to come down with that typhoid.'

While he was talking he eased around a little so he could see the jar sitting at Uncle Sagamore's side. He watched it like he was thinking of some big joke he wanted to remember.

'Well sir, that's real nice of the shurf,' Uncle Sagamore says. He looked at Pop. 'It's just like I was telling you, Sam. You take a lot of them goddamn lard-gutted politicians settin' around on their fat in the courthouse with both hands in the taxpayer's pocket, they don't do nothing to earn their money; but these shurf's boys is different. Now you take them, they're out protectin' the pore taxpayer, the way they ort to be, lookin' out for airplanes and forest fars and frettin' about this here typhoid and watchin' him through field glasses so he maybe don't fall down and die of sunstroke while he's out here workin' from sunup to dark to pay his taxes and keep the trough full for 'em. Makes a man downright proud to know they're on the job like that. So you boys just go on out there and draw up a bucket of that water and I'll see if I can find an old fruit jar or something you can put her in.'

'Oh, we wouldn't want to put you out,' the gold-tooth one says, and grins. 'We'll just take that jarful you got settin' there by your hip. That'll be plenty for the grand jury – I mean, the health department – to analyse.'

'Oh, you mean this one?' Uncle Sagamore says. He brought the jar out. 'Why, boys, this ain't well water.'

'It's *not*?' The two sheriff's men was so astonished they looked at each other again. 'Imagine that! It's not well water.'

'Why, no,' Uncle Sagamore says, 'this here is a kind of a remedy I seen advertised in one of them magazines. "Do You Feel Old at Forty!" it says, and here was this picture of this purty girl without much on in the way of clothes, and it goes on to say how you can get yore pep back and start shinin' up to the gals again if you been kind of losin' out on it lately, so I figure I ort to try me a little of it.'

'Well, what do you know?' the gold-tooth one says. 'And they sent it to you in a fruit jar, just like moon – I mean, well water?'

'Uh – not exactly,' Uncle Sagamore says. 'You see, you kind of make her up yourself. They send you this powder, whatever it is, and you mix it right at home. There may be just a teensy smell of alcohol about it, but don't let that fool you. It's just because the only thing I had to dissolve it in was some old patent medicine of Bessie's.'

'Well, imagine that!' the moustache one says. 'A little smell of alcohol. Who would of suspected a thing like that?'

The gold-tooth one picked the jar up and held it under his nose. The other one looked at him.

'Can't smell nothing with that stink out there,' he says. 'But, hell, we know what it is.'

'I tell you it's just a remedy, boys,' Uncle Sagamore says. 'You wouldn't want to take that in to the health department. They'd laugh at you.'

'Who do you think you're kiddin'?' the gold-tooth one says. 'But just to make sure it's evidence—' He tilted the jar up and took a swig out of it. He choked a little.

'How about it?' the other one asked.

The gold-tooth one looked kind of puzzled. 'I don't know. Strong enough to be moon, all right. But it's got a little funny taste. Here, see what you think.'

The moustache one looked a little doubtful. Then he says, 'Well, hell, he was drinkin' it.' So he tilted it up and swallowed.

He looked kind of puzzled too.

'See,' Uncle Sagamore says. 'I told you. It's just a remedy. But you boys is kind of young to be usin' it. You don't want to blame me if you start chasin' the gals around like banty roosters after a pullet when you get back to town.'

The gold-tooth one still looked a little doubtful. 'You can't kid me,' he says. 'I know moon when I taste it.' But he thought about it for a minute and then took another drink.

'Well, I don't know,' he says. 'It would be kind of silly if we took it in and it *was* medicine.'

'You ought to know better than to believe anything Sagamore Noonan says,' the moustache one told him. 'Here. Let me have it again.'

He took another one too. But he couldn't seem to make up his mind either.

'Well, take her in if you just got to,' Uncle Sagamore says. 'But you might as well set and visit a spell. Ain't no hurry.'

'No, we'll just run along,' they says. 'This was all we was after. Didn't want you to catch that typhoid.' They started to turn around.

Uncle Sagamore lifted the shotgun down kind of absent-minded and set it across his knees. He broke it, lifted the shells out and looked at them like he wanted to be sure they was really in it, and then slid 'em back in and closed the gun again. He was sliding the safety catch back and forth, just to be doing something, the way a man scribbles with a pencil while he's talking on the telephone. They watched him. The moustache one licked his lips.

'Sure you boys can't set a spell?' Uncle Sagamore asked. 'No use you rushin' off in the heat of the day.'

They stopped. The gold-tooth one says, 'Uh – well—'

'That's the trouble nowadays,' Uncle Sagamore went on. 'People just don't take the time to be neighbourly. Come a-chargin' in here like a highlifed shoat to save a man from comin' down with that typhoid, and then before he can hardly thank 'em for what they done they get another burr under their crupper and go tearin' off to hell an' gone to save some other pore taxpayer from something. Man was to just set once in a while he'd live longer.'

The two sheriff's men looked at each other again and then out at the car like it had suddenly got a long way off and they wasn't sure they could make it that far in the hot sun. They kind of oozed down on the steps, still watching Uncle Sagamore and looking into the end of the shotgun. 'Well, I reckon there' ain't no great hurry, come to think of it,' the gold-tooth one says.

'Now you're talkin',' Uncle Sagamore says. He took the old plug of tobacco out of his pocket, rubbed it on his overall leg to get off some of the lint and dirt and the roofing tack that was sticking to it, and bit off a big chew.

'Want to make you acquainted with my kinfolks,' he went on. 'This is my brother Sam and his boy. Sam's in the investment business in New York. Sam, say howdy to the shurf's boys. The high-pockets one with the chicken fat in his hair is Booger Ledbetter, and the other one, with that kiss-me-quick moustache, is Otis Sears.'

'Howdy,' Pop says.

'Howdy,' Booger says.

'Howdy,' Otis says.

Nobody said anything else for a minute or two. We all just sat there hunkered down looking at each other. I was on one side of Uncle Sagamore and Pop was on the other, and the two sheriff's men was on the top step, in front of us. I could hear that bug going buz-z-z-z out in the trees again. Then a little breeze come along and the smell got awful. The sheriff's men fanned harder with their hats.

'You boys warm?' Uncle Sagamore asked.

'Well, not exactly,' Booger says. 'It's just that smell. Get's sort of rank at times.'

'Smell?' Uncle Sagamore asked. He looked at them kind of puzzled, and then at Pop. 'You smell anything, Sam?'

Pop quit waving the air with his hat. 'Why, no,' he says, surprised like. 'What kind of a smell?'

Uncle Sagamore looked back at Booger and Otis. 'You sure you boys ain't just imaginin' it? Where does it seem to be coming from?'

'Why, I thought from the tubs over there,' Booger says.

'You don't mean my tannery, do you?' Uncle Sagamore asked.

'Well – uh,' Booger says, looking at the end of the shotgun again. 'I thought there was a sort of smell coming from over there, but maybe I was wrong.'

'Sure is funny,' Uncle Sagamore says. 'I ain't noticed a thing, myself. But I'm glad you boys mentioned it; reminds me it's time for them two on the end to dreen a little. They been soakin' for nine days now, and I better hang 'em up. I'll be right back.'

He got up with the shotgun under his arm and walked over to the end of the porch. He stepped down and lifted the old cowhide out of the end tub with a stick and threw it over the clothes line, kind of spreading it out. Then he took the next one out and spread it on the line too. They begin to drip brownish water onto the ground.

They was bad enough before, but now when they was out in the air it was awful. They was only ten or twelve feet away, and with the air circulating around 'em and then blowing over us in the little breeze I could feel my eyes watering and my breath choking up in my throat.

Booger and Otis was looking a little sick. They would breathe real slow and easy, and fan with their hats, and then they'd look at Uncle Sagamore and quit fanning and just try not to breathe any more than they had to.

Uncle Sagamore come back and sat down with his back against the door jamb and the shotgun over his knees. He didn't seem to notice the smell at all.

'I was kinda wantin' to show you boys my tannery,' he says. 'Bein' in the gov'ment, so to speak, you're probably interested in new industries and the like, and the different ways a man can scrabble around and break his back to make enough money to pay his taxes. What with them pussel-gutted politicians settin' around in the court-house just waitin' for him to scratch another nickel out of the ground, so they can swoop down on it like sparrows after a oat-foundered horse, a man's got to do something or he'd get desperate and start runnin' for office hisself. So I figured I'd go in the leather business as kind of a sideline.'

'Why, that sounds like a real good idea,' Otis says, wiping the sweat off his face.

Uncle Sagamore nodded his head. 'Sure. That way, I figure I might be able to eat something once in a while to stay alive so I can manage to get in town once a year to borrow enough money to make another crop, and kinda keep goin', so none of them fat bastards would ever have to do anything real desperate, like goin' to work. You couldn't have nothing like that. If them Rooshians ever heard things was so tough over here that politicians was goin' to work, they'd attack us in a minute.'

'Yeah, I reckon that's right,' Otis said, like he didn't really think so but figured he ought to say something just to be polite.

The conversation kind of died then and we all just sat there. You could see the heat waves dancing out along the hill, and once in a while there'd be some hammering from down where Uncle Finley was.

Pop nodded his head down that way, and asked Uncle Sagamore, 'Don't he ever knock off?'

Uncle Sagamore puckered up his lips and shot out a stream of tobacco juice. It sailed out flat and straight, right between Booger and Otis, and landed *ka-splott* in the yard.

'No,' he says. 'Only when he runs out of boards. Things is kind of slow right now, since he used up the last privy, but he manages to keep busy with a little patchin' here and there.'

We all looked at Uncle Finley.

'Just what's he building, anyway?' Pop asked.

'A boat,' Uncle Sagamore says.

'Boat?'

Uncle Sagamore nodded. 'That's right. The way Finley figures, it's going' to start rainin' like pourin' water out of a boot any day now. And when the day comes he's goin' to go sailin' off like a bug on a whiteoak chip and the rest of us sinful bastards is going to be drowned. He thought for a while of maybe takin' Bessie along, being she's his sister, but after she raised so much hell about the privies, he finally told her he'd takened it up with the Vision and the Vision says the hell with her, let her drowned like the rest of us.'

'What kind of a vision is this?' Pop asked.

I was sort of wishing he wouldn't keep asking about it, so we could maybe get off the porch and away from that smell, but it seemed like he was anxious to hear about it now and Uncle Sagamore was real anxious for all of us to stay there so he'd have somebody to talk to. Anyway, that's the way it looked, so I didn't say anything about wanting to move. Sig Freed was the only one that was comfortable. He went way off up the hill and laid down under a bush.

Well, not the only one. Uncle Sagamore seemed to be comfortable enough too. He stretched a little and scratched one leg with the big toenail on his other foot, and moved his tobacco into the other cheek.

'The Vision?' he says. 'Oh, Finley seen it one night about four years ago, as near as I can recollect. Me and Bessie was asleep in the front room when he come a-tearin' through the house in his nightshirt like somebody'd jabbed him in the butt with a bull nettle and says as how this Vision had told him he'd better not lose no time because the end of the world was due any minute. So he runs out in the back yard with a pinch bar and starts tearin' down the hen house to get boards to make this boat with. It was only about two o'clock in the morning, and there was a regular damn madhouse with all them chickens squawkin' and tryin' to figure out what's goin' on, and Bessie yellin' at Finley to go on back to bed. I didn't hardly get no rest at all.'

Four

'And he's been building her ever since?' Pop asked.

'Off and on,' Uncle Sagamore says. 'Dependin' on the supply of boards. After he used up the hen house and the shed I used to keep the truck in, he started to tear down the house, but we finally got him talked out of that. So then he starts driftin' around to the neighbours, pickin' up any boards that wasn't nailed down too tight. He tore down Marvin Jimerson's hawg pen so many times Marvin finally got a court order agin him and says if he has to chase them hawgs one more time he's comin' up here and shoot Finley right in the tail with a charge of rock salt, he don't care if Finley did used to be a preacher and was the one that baptised Miz Jimerson. Says come to thing of it, she takened the pneumonia when he baptised her anyhow.'

Pop was looking down the hill. 'Kinda leaky for a boat, ain't she?' he asked. 'You can see all the way through her in places.'

'Oh, that's on account of the privies,' Uncle Sagamore says. 'He's got seven of 'em in there now, if I ain't lost count. You see, every time Bessie leaves me, Finley rushes out there with his pinch bar and starts tarin' the privy apart before she's out of sight. He gets the planks all nailed into his boat, and about that time Bessie gets over her sull an' comes home, and I got to build a new one.'

'Bessie leaves you?' Pop asked. 'Is she gone now?'

'Oh, sure,' Uncle Sagamore says. 'Been gone a week last Sunday. She'll be back in about twelve days now. Last couple of years she's been stayin' away three weeks each time. Before that she always come home in ten days.'

'How's that?' Pop asked.

Uncle Sagamore scratched his leg with his toenail again and started to pucker up his lips like he was going to sail out some more tobacco juice. Booger and Otis watched him and kind of pulled back on each side like sliding doors opening. He didn't spit for a minute and they relaxed and straightened up a little, and then he spit and they had to jerk back real fast.

'Well, it's like this,' Uncle Sagamore says. 'Every once in a while, maybe twice a year, Bessie gets all galled under the britchin' about something and starts faunchin' around here sayin' she's takened all she can take, she just ain't goin' to put up with me no longer, ain't nobody could live with me. Usually over some triflin' little thing that don't amount to a hill of beans, like I won't wash my feet or something, but she gets all swole up like a snakebit pup and says she's leavin' me for good this time. So she packs her suitcase and gets her egg money and walks down to Jimerson's which is on the party line and calls Bud Watkins that runs the taxi in town, and Bud comes after her. She gets on the bus and goes down to Glencove to stay with her Cousin Viola, the one that married Vergil Talley.

'Well, I don't know if you recollect Cousin Viola, but you can't take too much of her at one time. She's kind of delicate and refined, only she's got this rumblin' in her stummick, an' every time her stummick rumbles she pats herself on the mouth with three fingers an' says, "Excuse me." Well, something like this all day long is bad enough, but on top of that she's got this damn gallstone.'

'Gallstone?' Pop asked.

'That's right,' Uncle Sagamore says. 'Six, eight years ago she had it takened out at the hospital, an' this fool doctor didn't have no better sense than to tell her it was the biggest one he ever seen, outside of one somebody takened out of a giraffe. Well, Viola was all set up about that, so she brought it home with her and put it in a little jar on the mantel an' took to tellin' people about it. One time, Vergil says, some people's car got stuck in the mud in front of the house an' they couldn't get away, an' Viola talked about that gallstone for thirteen hours and twenty minutes without stoppin'. Man finally give Vergil the keys to the car and said he'd be back for it in the summer when the roads dried out. People took to movin' out of the community rather than havin' to dodge her all the time, so when Bessie'd leave me an' go down there Viola'd be all primed and loaded for her. If Bessie was real mad at me she could hold out for ten days.'

Uncle Sagamore stopped talking and looked at Booger and Otis. They was shifting around on the step like they couldn't get comfortable anywhere.

'I ain't borin' you boys with all this, am I?' he asked.

'Why, no,' Booger says. ' – uh – that is—' He looked kind of funny. Pale, sort of, and sweating pretty heavy. His face was all slick and white. Otis was the same way. It didn't seem to be the smell that was bothering them, though, because they wasn't fanning with their hats any more. They just seemed to be kind of restless.

'Sure wouldn't want to get tiresome an' bore you boys,' Uncle Sagamore says. 'Especially after what you done, rushin' down here to save us from that typhoid an' all.'

'But how does it happen Bessie stays away three weeks now?' Pop asked. 'Is Viola beginning to run down, or something?'

'Oh,' Uncle Sagamore says. He sailed out some more tobacco juice, and wiped his mouth with the back of his hand. 'No. It was like this. Couple years ago, I reckon it was, Vergil made a pretty good cotton crop, an' they could see there was goin' to be money ahead even after they paid off the store. But before Vergil could get in to town to buy another secondhand Buick with it, Viola sneaked off to the hospital an' had about four hundred dollars' worth of new stuff takened out on the credit. Mostly female stuff I reckon; she'd never used it much because she ain't stopped talkin' long enough since they got married for Vergil to get her in the family way. I don't know why it is, but no matter how hard up a man is he ain't goin' to do his best with a woman that's talkin' five quarts to the gallon about her goddam gallstone.

'But, anyhow, I reckon Cousin Viola really shot the wad. Four hundred dollars' worth of stuff is a lot, especially since they already got you open an' you're gettin' wholesale rates after they write off the first slice or two. So if Vergil never made another good crop, she was set for life. It wasn't that she talked any less, but just that she had more to talk about now an' could kind of spread out over more ground. That's the reason Bessie's been stayin' three weeks lately, Viola don't hardly have to start repeatin' herself in less than that.'

Uncle Sagamore stopped again. You could see now that there was really something bothering Booger and Otis. Their eyes was big and kind of staring, like they hurt somewhere, and their faces was white as chalk, with big drops of sweat oozing out on their foreheads.

Uncle Sagamore looked around at Pop. 'Well sir, by golly, I get to ramblin' on like this, looks like I never know when to stop. I just remembered Billy asked me something while ago, an' I never did take time to answer him. What was it, now?'

Well, I couldn't remember anything like that, but I was beginning to learn about Uncle Sagamore. He wasn't talking to me. He'd asked Pop, so I stayed shut up. That was safest.

'Hmmmmm,' Pop says. 'He asked you what something was, as I recall.'

Uncle Sagamore nodded. 'Sure. I recollect now. He wanted

to know what croton oil was. Why you suppose he'd ask a fool thing—'

Booger and Otis stared at him with their eyes about to pop out. '*Croton oil*?' Booger says.

'*Croton oil*?' Otis says, in just the same way.

'Kids can ask some of the damnedest questions,' Uncle Sagamore went on. 'Without no reason at all.'

He pulled a big red handkerchief out of his overall pocket and started to mop the bald spot on his head. Some kind of black powder fell out of it. He looked at it, sort of puzzled.

'Now, how in the hell did black pepper get in my pocket?' he asked, like he was talking to hisself. 'Oh. I recollect now. I spilled some when I was gettin' breakfast. Atchooooo!'

Some of it got in my nose and I sneezed. Then Pop sneezed. And Uncle Sagamore sneezed again.

But Otis and Booger didn't sneeze. It was a little peculiar, the way they acted. Their eyes kept getting bigger and bigger, with that staring sort of horror in them, and they pressed fingers under their noses and breathed in real slow through their mouths. Then they both got full of air and it seemed like they couldn't breathe out. They clamped hands over their faces and tried to let the air escape a little at a time, kind of whining down in their throats.

One of 'em would say, 'A-ah-ah—' like he was about to sneeze, and he would clamp his mouth and nose shut with both hands and begin to turn purple in the face, with his eyes watering and sweat running down his forehead. It would pass, and he would let a little air out, and then the other one would start to go 'A-ah-ah—' and he'd go through the same thing.

Uncle Sagamore sneezed again. 'Damn that pepper, anyhow,' he says, and waved his handkerchief at it. It didn't do much good except to stir up what had already settled on the floor.

Booger and Otis grabbed their faces harder.

Uncle Sagamore shifted his tobacco into the other side of his face. 'Now, where was I?' he says. 'Oh, yes. About them privies. Well, Bessie raised hell with Finley the first few times for tearin' it down each time before she'd hardly got out of sight, but it didn't do no good except to get her scratched off the passenger list, like I said. Finley and the Vision kind of voted her out, you might say.

'So now when she gets a bellyful of Cousin Viola and comes home, as soon as she gets off the bus in town she goes right over to the E. M. Staggers Lumber Company and orders a bill of material for a new privy. They made up so many of 'em now they don't even have to figure it any more. Got a list all wrote out, right down to the last ten-penny nail, hangin' on a hook over the manager's desk. So they just load it on the truck an' Bessie rides out with 'em.'

But I wasn't listening to Uncle Sagamore now. I was watching Booger and Otis. They was still holding their faces like they was afraid they'd die of the pneumonia if they ever sneezed. All you could see was their eyes with that terrible staring in them. They looked at Uncle Sagamore and the end of the shotgun and then out towards the car like it was a million miles away. They couldn't sit still at all. They'd weave back and forth and kind of shift around on the step; but it was funny, each time they shifted they went backward a little. They slid down to the next step, and then the bottom one. They stood up and started easing away like they had something on their minds and had lost interest in Uncle Sagamore's story altogether.

They started out slow but began gathering speed, and by the time they got to the car they was really travelling. I never did figure out how they got the doors open and shot inside that fast, but by the time they'd hit the seat the car jumped ahead, making a long, looping turn with the tyres screaming, and they was headed back up the road towards the gate.

Uncle Sagamore looked at 'em, and sailed out some more tobacco juice. 'Doggone,' he says. 'I should of knowed I was borin' them boys.'

Just then the car hit one of those bumps and went up about three feet in the air. They must have put the brakes on while it was still off the ground, because when it hit it just slid kind of nose down, and turned crossways and stopped about half out of the road.

The doors flew open and Booger and Otis jumped out, one on each side, and started running towards the trees. They reminded me of horses coming out of a starting gate, the way they took off. Booger had to go around the car, so he was sort of left at the post, but as soon as he was clear and had racing room he went into a drive and started closing fast on Otis. Otis come on again, but Booger was laying up close to the pace now and he finally pulled into the lead by a good length and a half, and won going away. They shot into the trees.

Uncle Sagamore scratched his leg with his big toe again. 'Sure hope them boys ain't comin' down with that typhoid,' he says, and picked up the glass jar they had forgot to take along with them

34

to have analysed.

He reached it back through the door and traded it for the other one. He handed this one to Pop. They both took a drink.

Uncle Sagamore leaned the shotgun back against the wall and stretched. 'You know,' he says, 'that stuff might make a purty good remedy, at that. Even if it didn't help a man out none with the gals, it'd sure take his mind off 'em.'

Well, after Booger and Otis had come out of the trees and got back in their car and left, Uncle Sagamore backed his truck out of the shed down by the barn. Him and Pop loaded the tannery tubs on it and took them off in the timber back of the cornfield.

'Think they been in the sun long enough for now,' he says. 'This leather-makin' is ticklish business. Got to let it age just right, part of the time up there in the sun, and then down here in the shade for a few days.'

I wondered why they had to be clear up there beside the house just to be in the sun, but I didn't say anything. This didn't seem like much of a place for having your questions answered.

Uncle Sagamore and Pop talked it over about us staying there for the summer and Uncle Sagamore said it would be fine, only we'd have to kind of provision ourselves. He said he'd been so taken up with his tannery work this spring he'd forgot to plant any garden, and the chickens always quit laying when he brought his tubs up to the house to age in the sun.

'Oh, that's all right,' Pop says. 'We'll run into town right now and lay in some supplies.'

So we unhitched the trailer and left it there under the tree and started out in the car. When we passed Mr Jimerson's place he was lying on his back on the front porch. He waved a hand and grinned at us.

'Guess they didn't run over any of his hawgs this time,' Pop says.

'Why do you suppose they're always trying to save Uncle Sagamore from something?' I asked him.

'Well, he's a big taxpayer,' Pop says. 'And I reckon they just like him.'

It was about two more miles from there out to where the little road joined the highway. But just before we got there we came around a little curve and Pop slammed on the brakes and stopped. There was a car and a big, shiny, silver-and-blue house trailer pulled about half-way off the road.

Pop looked at it. We could get by all right, but it was a funny place to meet a big trailer like that because this road didn't go anywhere except to some farms like Uncle Sagamore's back towards the river bottom. And there was nobody in the car.

'They must be lost,' Pop says.

We got out and walked around it. The doors was closed and the curtains was pulled tight across the windows. We didn't hear anybody. It was quiet and peaceful there in the pine trees, except once in a while we could hear a car go past on the highway just around the next bend.

It was funny. The car and the trailer seemed to be all right, and they wasn't stuck in the sand or anything. It just looked like somebody had pulled it in here and then gone off and left it. We couldn't figure it out.

Then we saw the man.

He was down the road at the next bend, but was off a little to one side, in the trees. His back was to us, but he was standing real still among the trunks, watching the highway.

'Must be waiting for somebody,' Pop says.

Just then the man turned his head and saw us standing beside the trailer. He whirled around and started running towards us along the road. In spite of how hot it was, he had on a double-breasted flannel suit and was wearing a Panama hat and tan-and-white shoes. He kept watching us while he ran.

'What the hell are you looking for?' he barked at Pop when he came up.

Pop leaned against the side of our car. 'Why, we was just passin', and thought maybe you was in trouble, or something,' he says.

The man looked us over. Pop was dressed the way he always was around the tracks, in levis and old scuffed-up cowboy boots and a straw sombrero. It gives the clients, as Pop calls 'em, confidence to know the man they're dealing with is connected with a big gamble. In fact, that's the way he got his business name. Stablehand Noonan, he prints on top of the sheets. Anyway, when the man sized us up a little it seemed to give him confidence too, because he kind of cooled off.

'Oh,' he says. 'No. No trouble. I just stopped to cool off the motor.'

He lit a cigarette and kept on watching us like he was thinking of something. He was dark complected and had real cold blue eyes and a slim black moustache. His hair was black under the Panama hat. You could see he was hot inside that double-breasted flannel coat, and it looked funny out here among the pine trees. He carried his left arm a little awkward, out from his body somewhat, and when he raised his hands to light the cigarette the coat opened a crack at the top and I saw a narrow leather strap running across his chest. I figured he was wearing some kind of a brace. Maybe he'd had the polio.

'You live around here?' he asked Pop.

Pop nodded. 'Back up the road a piece. Me and my brother Sagamore own a big cotton plantation. You figure on visitin' back in that direction? Kinfolks, I mean?'

The man's eyes got narrow, like he was thinking. 'Not exactly,' he says. 'To tell you the truth, I was looking for a spot to camp for a few months. Some place where it was quiet and kinda off the beaten track, and a man wouldn't be bothered too much by the tourists.'

I could see Pop beginning to think too. 'Kind of a out-of-the-way place, you mean? Where you could sort of get away from the highway noise, an' just lay around, and maybe fish, without nobody to bother you?'

'That's it,' the man says. 'You know of a spot like that around here?'

'Well, I don't know,' Pop says. 'My brother Sagamore and me might be able to rent you a little campground. We got a lake in there, and lots of trees, but the place is kind of hard to get to and nobody ever goes in there.'

The man's face lit up. 'That sounds fine,' he says.

'No traffic at all,' Pop says. 'It's on a dead-end road. You alone?'

'Well, not exactly,' the man says. I noticed that all the time he was talking he kept looking around every few seconds to watch that bend of the road. 'I've got my niece with me.'

'Niece?' Pop asked.

The man nodded. 'Let's get out of this hot sun.' He moved out of the road and we all went over and squatted down in the shade of the pine trees on the other side of the trailer. He faced so he could watch towards the highway.

He took another drag on his cigarette and tossed it away, and nodded towards the trailer. 'Maybe I better introduce myself,' he says. 'I'm Dr Severance. I'm a specialist in nervous disorders and anaemia. My niece, Miss Harrington, is in there. It's on her account I'm looking for a secluded place to camp. She's an invalid, and under my care. She needs a long rest, in quiet surroundings.'

'I see,' Pop says.

'You understand,' the man went on, 'I'm telling you this in the strictest confidence. Miss Harrington is from a very old and very wealthy New Orleans family. She's a delicate and very sensitive girl who's in bad health and has to have absolute rest and quiet for a long time. Her fiancé was killed in an automobile crash this spring, and she suffered a nervous breakdown which finally turned into this rare type of anaemia. She's been given up by specialists all over the United States and Europe, so in desperation I finally turned my New York practice over to my assistants and took on the case myself. In all medical history there've been only three cases of it, and it's supposed to be incurable, but it just happened I'd once read an obscure article by Von Hofbrau, the Austrian anaemia specialist—'

The man stopped and shook his head. 'But there's no use bothering you with all this medical stuff. The point is that Miss Harrington has to have perfect seclusion, and lots of fresh leafy vegetables and eggs, and outdoor air, and she can't be disturbed by her family and reporters all the time. So if you think your farm will fill the bill—'

'Oh, sure,' Pop says. 'A farm is just what you want. We got slathers of fresh vegetables and eggs, and absolute quiet. Now as to the price—'

Dr Severance waved a hand. 'Anything. Anything within reason.'

Pop looked at his clothes and then at the car and the trailer. 'Say fif — I mean sixty dollars a month?'

'Quite all right,' Dr Severance says. He patted his pocket. 'Wait'll I get another pack of cigarettes out of the car.'

He got up and walked around in front of the trailer.

Pop shook his head kind of sad and looked at me. 'That's the hell of it,' he says. 'You get out of touch for even a week and you begin to lose the knack and can't tell within fifty dollars what a client'll go for.'

Dr Severance came back opening a package of cigarettes.

'You understand, of course,' Pop says, 'that's per head. Since there's two of you it'll be a hundred and twenty.'

Dr Severance looked at Pop's levis and straw sombrero again and says, 'Hmmm.' Then he shrugged his shoulders. 'Well, that's all right. Provided the place is what you say it is.'

Pop started to say something, and then just stopped with his mouth hanging open.

The door of the trailer had opened, and a girl was standing in the doorway looking out at us. She was tall and dark-haired, with bright red lips and blue eyes, and she didn't have anything on but a sort of romper affair which was just a pair of short white pants and this kind of halter thing around her bosom. The pants didn't cover hardly any of her long legs.

Her hair was tousled a little, like she'd just got up, and she had a long cigarette in her hand. She sure was pretty.

She had a big bosom, as big as a Welfare lady's, but she was a lot younger, of course. Somehow she made you think of a real, real ripe peach, the way she filled up those little pants and that bosom thing and stuck out of 'em all pink and smooth in every direction.

Pop said, 'Ho-ly hell,' real low, like he was talking to hisself.

She looked at all of us, and said to Dr Severance, 'What's all this convention of hay-shakers?'

Dr Severance nodded towards her. 'My niece, Miss Harrington,' he says. 'I'd like you to meet Mr – uh—'

Pop kind of shook himself, like he was coming out of a trance. 'Oh,' he says, 'Noonan, lady. Sam Noonan.'

Miss Harrington waved the cigarette at him. 'Hi, dad,' she says. 'Reel in your tongue. You're getting your shirt wet.'

Five

Dr Severance's eyes was colder than ever. 'Pamela,' he says, 'I thought I told you to stay inside the trailer. Remember your anaemia.'

'Relax,' Miss Harrington says. 'It's too damned hot in there.'

She sat down in the doorway and stretched out her legs. She took a puff on her cigarette, looked at her legs, and then at Pop. 'What's the matter, Zeke? Am I hurt somewhere?'

'Oh,' Pop says, 'Uh – no. I just thought for a minute your face was kind of familiar.'

'How would you know?' Miss Harrington asked.

'I was sure sorry to hear about your anaemia,' Pop says.

'That's sweet of you.'

Dr Severance butted in. 'Miss Harrington's anaemia is the very worst kind. It doesn't show. That's what makes it so hard to diagnose and cure. Just looking at her you wouldn't think she had anything, would you?'

'Well, I wouldn't say that,' Pop says.

'Look,' Miss Harrington says to the doctor, 'what's with this Hiram type, anyway? We going to adopt him, or something? Tell him to go fry a hush-puppy and let's get the hell out of here.'

'Keep your shirt on,' Dr Severance told her. 'Mr Noonan is going to rent us a camping place on his farm.'

Miss Harrington yawned. 'Well, goody.'

'You'll have absolute rest and quiet, and lots of fresh leafy vegetables.'

'Just what I always wanted,' she says.

Pop stood up. 'We got to drive in to town to buy some groceries,' he told the doctor. 'It won't take long, so you just wait here and when we come back we'll lead you to the farm.'

Dr Severance came around the trailer with us, and when we got in the car he put his arms on the door and leaned in a little. He jerked his head towards the trailer.

'When you're in town,' he says to Pop, 'maybe it would be a good idea if you didn't say anything about Miss Harrington to anybody. You know how the word gets around, and I wouldn't want her pestered by a flock of reporters all the time.'

'We won't say a word,' Pop says. He turned the key to the ignition, and then he asked, 'By the way, this anaemia's not catching, is it?'

Dr Severance shook his head. 'No. It's hardly contagious at all. The only way you can catch it is if you actually touch somebody who's got it.' He stopped, and then took a long look at Pop's face. 'And of course you got better sense than to do a crazy thing like that.'

'Now that you brought it up,' Pop says, 'I sure have.'

We drove on around the bend and out onto the highway. It was only five miles from there to town. Pop was sort of quiet, except that every once in a while he would say, 'My God,' like he was talking to hisself.

'Miss Harrington's nice,' I says to him. 'You don't suppose she's with the Welfare, do you?'

'I doubt it,' Pop says.

'I didn't think so,' I says. 'But she has got kind of a Welfare bosom.'

Pop didn't act like he even heard me. His hands was gripping the wheel real hard and he was staring straight ahead.

'My God,' he says again. The car swerved across the road and almost went in the ditch on the wrong side. He yanked the wheel and we straightened out again.

'You oughtn't to talk about Miss Harrington's bosom,' he says to me like he was mad. 'The poor girl's not well. She's got the anaemia.'

'Is that bad, Pop?' I asked.

'Well,' he says, 'I can't see that it's done her much harm so far, but I reckon it's pretty serious if you got to eat vegetables for it.'

We got into town. It was a pretty little town, with a red brick courthouse in a square and big trees growing all around. We parked the car in the square and went into a grocery store. Pop bought eight pounds of baloney and six loaves of bread, and then he got a couple cases of beer and some cigars. I asked him if I could have a candy bar. He said they was bad for my teeth, but finally give in and bought me one. We went back out and got in the car.

We was just about to drive off when Pop suddenly remembered something. 'I almost forgot,' he says. 'We're all out of hawg lard. I got to get some to fry the baloney in.'

He went back in the grocery store. I sat in the car, finishing my candy bar and looking out at the square. It was just then that I saw the big car go by with the men in it wearing Panama hats. There was three of them, and they all had on double-breasted flannel suits like Dr. Severance's. The car had Louisiana licence plates, like his did, and it was just going along real slow while the men looked around. They kept watching the sidewalks and the other cars.

They went on around the square, and in a few minutes they came by again. There was a parking place ahead of us, and they pulled in and got out and started into the restaurant next to the grocery store. They walked close together, watching the other people all the time, and I noticed they all had that awkward way of carrying their left arm, just like Dr Severance had.

Just then Pop came out of the grocery store carrying the can of hog lard, and he nearly bumped into them. He stopped real quick and stared at them.

The one on that side turned his face a little and said to him out of the corner of his mouth, 'You looking for somebody, Jack?'

Pop sort of swallowed, and says, 'No. Nobody at all.' He hurried across the sidewalk and got into the car, and we shot out of the parking place. The three men went on into the café.

As we drove out of town I said to Pop, 'They looked a little like Dr Severance, didn't they?'

'Yeah,' he says. 'Maybe there's a doctor's convention in town.'

When we got back, Dr Severance was still waiting there around the bend from the highway. I didn't see Miss Harrington anywhere, so she had probably gone back in the trailer. Pop told the doctor to follow us, and we started off.

It was only about two miles, and the big car didn't have any trouble pulling the trailer in the sand, so it wasn't too long till we came to the wire gate and turned off down the hill towards Uncle Sagamore's farmhouse. About a hundred yards before we got to the house Pop pulled off to the left and stopped among some big trees in a little level place looking out over the lake. He motioned for Dr Severance to stop. We all got out.

'Well, how does this strike you?' Pop asked the doctor.

Dr Severance looked all around and back up the hill towards the wire gate and the road. You couldn't see them from here because of the trees. 'Hmmmm,' he says. 'Seems to be all right.'

He took some money out of his wallet and gave it to Pop.

'Here's a month in advance,' he says. 'But I was just thinking. Maybe you'd better not mention anything about us being here. Around to the neighbours, I mean. There might be zoning restrictions against trailers.'

'That's right,' Pop says. 'I hadn't thought of that. We won't say a word.'

I saw Uncle Sagamore come out of the house and look up the hill towards us and start walking this way to find out what was going on. But just then I heard another car coming down the hill from the gate. From the sound of it, it was really travelling. It shot out of the trees and went bucking down towards the house just the way those two sheriffs' had. A big cloud of dust was boiling up behind it.

Then I forgot about it, watching Dr Severance. We was all three standing in front of his car when the other one shot out of the trees, but then he let out an awful cuss word and moved faster than I'd ever seen anybody move before. He whirled around and ducked behind the car so just his head was peering over, and his right hand shot up inside his coat. It all happened so fast I just stared at him.

The car went on past, bucking like crazy over the bumps. It slammed on down the hill and the man that was in it put his brakes on and it slid to a stop right by Uncle Sagamore. Dr Severance watched it, and then he straightened up. He looked around at us, and his eyes was real cold again.

'Who was that?' he barked at Pop.

'Uh—' Pop says. 'Just one of the neighbours. Probably wants to borrow something.'

'Oh,' Dr Severance said. He seemed to relax a little. 'I was afraid it was those damn reporters.'

Then he noticed he still had his hand inside his coat. He took it out, and shook his head. 'Heart twinge,' he said. 'Grabs me right there every once in a while.'

'Why, that's too bad,' Pop says. 'What you want to do is take it real easy and not excite yourself.' Then he grinned and scratched his head. 'But who am I to be prescribin' for a doctor?'

We all looked down the hill towards the house. There was only one man in the car. He got out and started talking to Uncle Sagamore, waving his arms like he was worked up about something.

Pop says to Dr Severance, 'Well, you go ahead and set up camp. I'll tell my brother Sagamore about our dicker.'

We drove down and parked under the big tree again, and walked over to where the man was still talking to Uncle Sagamore by his car. Or maybe talking wasn't just the word. I couldn't make out whether he was yelling or preaching, the way he was carrying on. He was a short, fat man with a big hat and a white moustache, and his face was as red as a beet. He was throwing his hands around, and every few seconds he would pull an arm across his face to wipe the sweat off.

Just as we walked up he took off his hat and pulled a big red handkerchief out of his pocket to mop his forehead, only he forgot which was which and mopped his face with the hat and got it all wadded up. When he saw what he had done he cussed something awful and threw the handkerchief on the ground and stomped on it with his cowboy boots and clapped the hat back on his head crossways and all smashed in. He was real excitable.

Uncle Sagamore just leaned against the side of the car and listened to him. Every once in a while he would pucker up his mouth and sail out some tobacco juice.

'What I want to know is what you done to them two deputies of mine!' the fat man was shouting. 'I can't get either one of 'em to hold still long enough to tell me what's wrong with him. The last time they was out here you damn near blowed 'em up with dynamite, and now they just keep chasin' each other down the hall to the john all gaunted down to skin an' bones like a blind muley-cow with the scours, and I can't get no sense out of 'em at all except one of 'em said he thought they'd been drinkin' croton oil.'

Uncle Sagamore just looked at him, real surprised. 'Croton oil?' he says, like he couldn't even believe it. 'Why, Shurf, they must of been just hoorawin' you. They wouldn't do nothin' like that. Why, you take a couple of men that's smart enough to get to be politicians an' draw a paycheck for settin' in the shade of the courthouse to watch out for gals gettin' in and out of cars so they don't sunburn their legs – why they got more sense than to drink croton oil.'

He stopped to sail out some more tobacco juice. The sheriff was just sputtering, like he couldn't even think of words any more.

Uncle Sagamore wiped his mouth with the back of his hand. 'Why, hell,' he says, 'even a old boll weevil like me that ain't got brains enough to do nothin' but work nineteen hours a day to pay his taxes is got more sense than to drink croton oil. It'll give you the scours something awful. But I'll tell you what, Shurf,' he went on. 'I won't let on to nobody that you even mentioned it. It would be a awful thing to get around, come to think of it, people sayin' to each other how them goddam fat politicians was gettin' so bored with high livin' and doin' nothing but milkin' the tax-payers that they've took to drinkin' croton oil just to pass the time. I won't breathe it to a soul.'

Uncle Sagamore looked around then and saw us. 'Shurf,' he says, 'I'd like to have you meet my brother Sam.'

The sheriff jerked his head around and stared at us. 'Oh, no!' he says, like he hurt somewhere. 'Oh, Jesus, no! Not two of you! Not two Noonans in the same county. God wouldn't do that to anybody. I'll – I'll—' He choked all up.

'Sam,' Uncle Sagamore went on, 'the shurf here is kind of worried about his men. Seems like they've started sneakin' off to drink croton oil on the sly, like a baby stuffin' beans up his nose, and he's afraid the voters'll get wind of it. But I was just tellin' him he ain't got a thing to worry about as far as we're concerned.

We can keep a secret as well as anybody in the county.'

'We sure can,' Pop says. 'Nobody'll ever find it out from us. But ain't that kind of a funny thing for 'em to want to do?'

'Well, sir,' Uncle Sagamore says, 'we're not in no position to judge, Sam. We're not in politics. Ain't no way we can rightly tell what kind of a strain a man might be under, settin' there every day with all that responsibility. Why, a strain like that could get so bad after a while a man might even start to think about gettin' out of politics and goin' to work, though offhand I can't seem to recollect of a case of one ever crackin' up quite as bad as that.'

The sheriff was getting a little purple around the face now. He kept trying to talk, but it was mainly just sputter, like steam pushing up the lid of a coffee pot. 'Sagamore Noonan!' he yells, 'I – I—'

Uncle Sagamore didn't even seem to hear him. He just shifted his tobacco over on the other side and shook his head sort of sad. 'Politics is hard on a man, Sam,' he says. 'It always puts me in mind of Bessie's cousin, Peebles. Peebles was a dep'ty shurf for a long time, till he begin to grow this here sort of mildew on his hunkers. Just regular mildew, like you see on a pone of bread that's got stale. It was a real puzzling thing, and they couldn't figure it out at all.

'Well sir, it went on like that for quite a spell, with Peebles goin' to the doctor every week or so to have this mildew scraped off his butt, but they never could figure out what caused it, till one day the doctor happened to be goin' by the courthouse durin' office hours an' he seen what it was. Seems like they'd put in one of them new-fangled sprinklin' systems on the lawn, and the edge of one of the sprays, by golly, reached over just to the edge of Peebles's settin' place on the step. Well, they got to inquirin' around, and found out that Peebles had been home sick the day they'd put in the sprinkler and tried it out, and they'd forgot to allow for him. So he'd been settin' there all these months with his tail in that spray of water.'

The sheriff seemed to get hold of hisself at last. His face was still purple, but he got real quiet. He reached down for his handkerchief and mopped his face sort of slow and deliberate; then he took a deep breath and put the handkerchief in his pocket and walked over in front of Uncle Sagamore like a man that was holding onto hisself real hard to keep from blowing up like a stick of dynamite. He began talking.

'Sagamore Noonan,' he says, real quiet, but still taking those deep breaths, 'when the voters elected me sheriff for the first time ten years ago I promised 'em I was going to make this county a decent place to live in by puttin' you so far back in the pen it'd cost you eight dollars to send a postcard out to the front gate. When they re-elected me six years ago, and then again two years ago, I promised 'em the same thing. They knew I was honestly tryin', and they believed me. They had patience, because they knew what I was up against.

'I'm still tryin'. And some day I'm going to do it. Some day I'm going to get enough evidence on you to send you up the river so far your grandchildren will be old men when you get back, and we can hold up our heads around here and look the rest of the state in the face.

'Sometimes I'm tempted to quit, to just throw up the job and sell my home and go somewhere else and start over, but then I get to thinkin' about all the other poor people in this county who'd have to stay here and go on putting up with you because they can't sell out and leave, so I stick it out and keep trying. It's an obligation, I reckon. I just can't abandon all these defenceless people to you.

'It ain't just a job. It's gone beyond that. I went into the Treasurer's office the other day and told 'em they didn't have to issue my pay-checks any more till I freed the county of you, and that if the people didn't re-elect me two years from this fall I'd go on servin' for nothing, right along with the new sheriff, till we got the evidence on you to put you away and we wouldn't be ashamed to bring innocent children into a world where you was running around loose.

'And now that I find out there ain't only you, that there's two of you here on this one farm with decent, God-fearin' people livin' all around you, I'm almost tempted to call the Governor and have him declare martial law. There must be something on the statute books to protect the citizens from you without havin' to go to court with evidence of any one particular crime.'

'It's like I was tellin' you, Sam,' Uncle Sagamore says. 'This shurf is a real fine man, aside from being a little inclined to get all het up over triflin' little things that don't amount to a hill of beans. Reckon he's got the high blood pressure. An' then, too, it must be kind of trying, havin' your men sneakin' around pokin' beans up their nose when you ain't lookin'.'

'No,' Pop says. 'They wasn't poking beans up their nose. They were drinking croton oil, remember?'

'Oh, sure,' Uncle Sagamore says. 'It was croton oil, wasn't it?'

The sheriff brought both hands up and rubbed 'em across his face, and he didn't say anything for a minute. He breathed kind of slow and heavy, but when he took his hands away he was still quiet.

'While I'm out here,' he says to Uncle Sagamore, 'I'm going to have a look in your barn. We been gettin' reports from various towns that you been doing a little shopping here and there.'

'Why, sure, Shurf,' Uncle Sagamore says. 'Help yourself. I'm always kind of proud when I done a little shopping. The way I see it, it shows good management when a man can have a little money left over to buy something for hisself after he's fed all the goddam politicians he's got lyin' in his lap.'

'Come on!' the sheriff says, real cold.

The barn was made out of logs, with split shingles for a roof. Inside there was some stalls for the mules. It was kind of dim, and smelled nice, just like the stables at a race track. In one corner there was a corncrib with a little door made out of planks.

We all stopped, and the sheriff went over and opened the corncrib door. 'Well, well,' he says, rubbing his hands together. 'Just like I thought.'

I couldn't see past him very well, but it looked like a lot of sacks of something or other piled up five or six feet high.

'Sure is a lot of awful sweet mule feed,' the sheriff says. He started counting, pointing with his finger and moving his lips. Uncle Sagamore leaned against the wall and sailed out some tobacco juice.

The sheriff finished counting. He turned around and looked at Uncle Sagamore, and he seemed to feel a lot better. 'Ninety sacks,' he says. 'That's about the way we heard it. That was quite a little shopping you did, here and there.'

'Well, you know how it is,' Uncle Sagamore says. 'A man's workin' eighteen, twenty hours a day, he don't get to town very often.'

'You mind lettin' me in on what you're aimin' to do with all of it?' the sheriff asked. 'Stories like that interest me.'

'Why, no. Not at all, Shurf,' Uncle Sagamore says. 'You see, when Sam here wrote me he was comin' to visit a spell this summer and was bringin' his boy, I figured I ort to lay in a little sweetnin'. You know how boys is. They got a sweet tooth.'

'Nine thousand pounds of sugar?' the sheriff asked. 'They must figure on staying several weeks. Ain't you afraid that much'd be bad for his teeth?'

Uncle Sagamore snapped his fingers. 'Well sir,' he says, 'you know, I never thought of that.'

The sheriff's face started to get purple again.

Uncle Sagamore shook his head, kind of sad. 'Imagine that,' he says. 'Sure looks like the joke's on me, buyin' all that sugar for nothin'.'

Six

We walked back to the car. The sheriff opened the door and started to get in. 'Well, you just go right ahead bein' smart, Sagamore Noonan,' he says. 'Sooner or later you're goin' to laugh on the other side of your face. It's here on this land, and we're goin' to find it. It ain't goin' to be so funny then.'

'Why, did you lose something, Shurf?' Uncle Sagamore asked. 'You should have told me. Any way me an' Sam can help, you just let us know. And don't you fret none about us tellin' anybody your men's started drinkin' croton oil. You can depend on us.'

The sheriff said a bad cuss word and got in and slammed the door. The car jumped ahead and made a big turn and then went bucking up the hill. It seemed like him and his men was always in a hurry. I thought it wasn't any wonder they kept running over Mr Jimerson's hogs.

I wondered why Uncle Sagamore had bought all that sugar, but I figured there wasn't any use asking him. Maybe I could ask Pop about it later. He might know. But I was sure he hadn't bought it on account of us, like he'd told the sheriff, because he didn't even know we was coming until we'd got here.

Uncle Sagamore looked up the hill to where you could just see Dr Severance's trailer in the edge of the trees. Pop remembered then that what with that excitable sheriff talking so much he'd forgot to tell Uncle Sagamore about it. So he told him.

'Well, is that a fact? A hundred and twenty a month,' Uncle Sagamore says, aiming some tobacco juice at a grasshopper about ten feet away on the sand. He missed him a couple inches. The grasshopper went away, buzzing. 'Got the anaemia, has she?'

'That's right,' Pop says. 'She has to eat vegetables.'

'Well sir, that's a shame,' Uncle Sagamore says. 'A young girl, and all.'

'By the way, have we got any vegetables?' Pop asked.

'Hmmm,' Uncle Sagamore says. 'I reckon there's still some of Bessie's turnips out there if the hawgs ain't rooted 'em all out.'

'Well, they ought to do fine,' Pop says. 'Come to think of it, whoever seen a hawg with the anaemia?'

We walked up the hill towards the trailer. It was getting along late in the afternoon now and the shadows of the trees was lengthening out and it was pretty out over the lake.

Dr Severance had uncoupled the trailer from the car and set up a striped canvas shade over the door like a front porch. There was a couple of canvas chairs and a little table under it, and a portable radio on the table was playing music. It was all real nice.

Just as we walked up Dr Severance came out the door. 'Hello,' he says to Pop, and Pop introduced him to Uncle Sagamore. He still had on the double-breasted suit, but he'd took off his tie and had a glass in his hand with ice and some stuff in it.

'Would you men care for a drink?' he asked.

'Why, if'n it wouldn't put you out,' Uncle Sagamore says.

He went back inside and we all hunkered down in the shade. We could hear him in the trailer clinking glasses and ice. And just then Miss Harrington came out the door.

'Well, ho-ly hell!' Uncle Sagamore says, just the way Pop had the other time.

She had changed clothes, but this little two-piece romper out-fit was just like the other one except that instead of being white it was striped like candy. She had on gold-coloured sandals with a strap that went between her toes, and her toenails was all painted gold. On her wrist was a big heavy bracelet, and one ankle had a thin gold chain around it. She rattled the ice in the glass she was carrying, and leaned against the door and looked at Uncle Sagamore.

'Does he hurt somewhere?' she asked Pop.

'Oh,' Pop says. 'This here is my brother Sagamore.'

'Well, I might have guessed that,' she says. 'There is something about the way he looks, if you know what I mean.'

Uncle Sagamore didn't say anything. He just went on staring. She snapped her fingers at him. 'Break it up, dad,' she says.

She sauntered out the door and sat down in one of the canvas chairs and crossed her legs.

'God, this is really back in the jungle,' she said.

'Fine climate, though,' Pop says. 'Best place in the world for anaemia.'

'Well, that's fine,' Miss Harrington said. She brushed a gnat off her leg, and looked at Uncle Sagamore again. 'If you run across anything you're not sure about, Zeb, don't hesitate to ask me.'

'Well sir,' Uncle Sagamore says to Pop, 'I reckon this is the first time I ever met up with the anaemia. You don't suppose Bessie'd be likely to catch it?'

'I reckon not,' Pop says. 'She's probably done past the age when she's apt to come down with it.'

Just then Dr Severance came out with the two drinks. He gave them to Pop and Uncle Sagamore and sat down in the other chair.

'Well, here's to Miss Harrington's recovery,' he says, and they all raised their glasses and drank.

Uncle Sagamore looked in his glass, and then says to Pop, 'He must of spilled some water in it.' He fished the ice out with his fingers and threw it away.

Dr Severance fiddled with the radio dial. 'I keep trying to pick up a New Orleans station,' he says. 'Miss Harrington gets home-sick, and it would make her feel better to hear a familiar voice. It's hard on a young girl, being torn away from her family and the social whirl of a big city like that, because of illness.'

The music stopped. He hit a new station, and a man's voice was talking: '*And now for the local news,*' it said. '*Police reported today there have been no new developments in the sensational gangland killing of Vincent (Tiger) Lilly which shook the city a week ago. The prosecution's star witness is still reported to be—*'

He turned the dial again and some more music came on. 'But this place is going to be wonderful for her,' he went on. 'It's just what I was hoping to find when I took charge of the case. She can get the rest her condition calls for. You gentlemen probably don't realise the absolutely man-killing social pace a debutante like Miss Harrington has to keep up with. Parties, balls, receptions, charity bazaars – it never lets up for a minute. I tell you, going through medical school is a cinch compared with it.'

Miss Harrington nodded. 'It's rough, MacDuff.'

'And with that anaemia sapping her strength by the hour,'

Dr Severance went on, 'well, it was killing her, that's all.'

Miss Harrington finished her drink and put the glass down on the table. She got up and walked down to the end of the trailer where you could see out over the lake.

She kind of swung and swayed when she walked, and Pop and Uncle Sagamore watched her real anxious like they was afraid she might fall or something.

Dr Severance went on talking what hard work it was being a debutante, whatever that was. Miss Harrington stood looking out over the lake, and I figured she was probably homesick all right, and lonesome. I liked her, because you could see she was real nice and she wasn't always wanting to grab a-hold of you and make a fuss like them Welfare ladies, so I felt sorry for her and wished she didn't have the anaemia and have to go away from home like that, and eat vegetables.

Just then the radio changed to another tune, a real pretty one that made you want to tap your feet. Miss Harrington was still looking the other way, but you could tell she heard it because she started moving her feet in time with it and swaying her body like she was going to dance. It was real pretty to see.

Dr Severance was still talking and didn't notice, but Uncle Sagamore and Pop was watching her real close. She swung around in her dancing, but it didn't seem like she even saw us. She had a faraway look in her eyes and you could tell she was humming the tune. Then she swung back facing the other way, and doggone if she didn't reach up behind her back and unsnap the ends of that bosom thing she was wearing.

As it came off she took one end of it in her hand and waved it like a streamer while she swayed back and forth in time to the music. She was still faced the other way, but you could see she didn't have nothing on but them little candy-striped pants. Then she turned back towards us, and as she did she caught up the bosom thing and held it pressed to her with one arm where it would have been if she was still wearing it, smiling kind of dreamy like, and I could hear her singing the words of the song.

She had a real nice voice.

Well, Pop and Uncle Sagamore was just enchanted with it, it was such a pretty dance. They leaned forward on their hunkers till they like to fell over, with their eyes bugged out, and the drinks in their hands was spilling on the ground. Miss Harrington swung on around away from us again and as she did she pulled the bosom thing away once more and started waving it in her hand like she was directing the orchestra.

Pop dropped his glass on the ground. He started to clap his hands, but then he caught hisself and looked at Dr Severance and didn't. But just then the doctor noticed the funny expressions on their faces and glanced around and saw Miss Harrington's dance.

He jumped half out of his chair and knocked his drink over. His eyes were cold as ice. He clapped his hands together real hard and yelled. 'Choo-Choo! Uh – *Pamela!*'

She jumped, and looked around, like she'd just remembered where she was. 'Oh,' she says, slipping the bosom thing back on. 'I wish they wouldn't play that.'

Dr Severance glared at her. She came over and picked up her glass and went inside the trailer to get a drink.

As soon as she went in the door Dr Severance looked at Pop and Uncle Sagamore and sighed, and shook his head real sad. 'There you are, gentlemen,' he says. 'That's what a nervous breakdown will do for you. Some people will try to tell you it's no worse than a bad cold, but you saw it with your own eyes. Her mind just stopped dead there for a minute and she was lost, and the only thing she could grab hold of was clear back in her childhood. All the little girls in her social set had to go to dancing school and take ballet lessons.' He shook his head again.

'Well, that's too bad,' Pop says. 'It sure is a shame. But you can see she's had a lot of trainin'. She might have made a great dancer.'

Uncle Sagamore nodded too. 'She sure has got the knack.'

When Miss Harrington came back she had two drinks with her. She walked over to where I was and smiled down at me. 'What's your name, junior?' she asked.

'Billy, ma'am,' I says.

'Well, Billy, they seem to have left you out when they passed the drinks around, so I brought you a coke.' She handed me the glass, and says, 'Why don't you and me walk down to the lake and see if it looks good to swim in?'

'Why, it's fine swimmin',' Pop says. 'As a matter of fact, I was just thinkin' I might be able to spare a little time off from work, an' teach you.'

'Down, boy,' Miss Harrington says. 'I already know how to swim. And I know all about being taught.'

She went back in the trailer and in a minute she came out with her handbag slung over her shoulder. We finished our drinks and went down through the trees towards the lake.

Uncle Sagamore and Pop started to get up like they wanted to come too, but Dr Severance shook his head at them and says, 'Boys, I wouldn't. Why don't you just stick around and talk?'

When we came out in the open we was right close to where Uncle Finley was working on his boat. Miss Harrington stopped and looked at it and at him hammering away up on his scaffold.

'What in the name of God is that?' she asked.

I told her about Uncle Finley and the Vision and how they figured all the sinners was going to drown when the rain started.

'Well, they sure got some ripe ones around here,' she says.

We started to go on past, and just then Uncle Finley looked around from his hammering and saw us. He just ignored us, like he had me and Pop, and took another swing at the nail with his hammer. Then all of a sudden he jumped and jerked his head around again and stared at Miss Harrington like he hadn't really seen her the first time.

He waved the hammer at her. 'Jezebel!' he yelled.

Miss Harrington stopped. She looked at him and then at me. 'Well, what bit him?' she asked.

Uncle Finley walked along the scaffold towards us, still craning his neck at her and pointing with his hammer. 'Bare naked Jezebel!' he says, furious like. 'Paradin' around here with your legs a-showin', and causin' sin.'

'Oh, crawl back in your fruit cake,' Miss Harrington says to him.

'He can't hear you,' I says. 'He's deaf as a post.'

We started to go on. Uncle Finley kept walking along the scaffold looking at Miss Harrington's legs and yelling, 'Jezebel,' and when he came to the end of it he didn't even notice. He just walked right off into thin air.

Lucky he dropped the hammer and managed to grab the side of the boat, or he'd have fell about six feet and likely hurt hisself. When we went on he was still hanging there with his face against the planks yelling, 'Sinful, naked hussy—' and trying to turn his head so he could see.

We walked on down to the edge of the lake. There wasn't any trees right here. There was a little sandy beach and the water looked shallow close to the shore. Further along there was trees on both sides, and up about a furlong the lake bent to the left and went out of sight around a point. The water was still, and you could see the trees reflected in it. It was real pretty.

Miss Harrington looked around and then back at Uncle Finley's boat and the house. 'If we want to swim,' she says, 'we'll have to get further away from the bald-headed row.'

'Have you got a bathing suit?' I asked.

'Well – yes,' she says.

'Why don't you go back and get it?' I said. 'And we can go on up to that point and go swimming now.'

'Oh, I've got it with me,' she said. 'It's here in my purse.'

'Well, fine,' I says.

We walked on around the edge of the lake and into the trees. In a little while we passed the point where the lake turned left and when we walked out to the edge of the water we was out of sight of the house and everything. It was nice. The lake was about fifty yards wide here, and the trees made shadows clear across it now that the sun was about to go down. It was real quiet and peaceful.

'Do you reckon it's too deep close to shore?' I asked. 'I don't know how to swim.'

'No,' she says. 'I think we can wade out. And I'll help you. But you wait till I can change into my suit.'

She went into some bushes and ferns that was growing along the bank off to the left. I stripped down to my boxer shorts and waited for her. It looked like a fine place to swim, and I was anxious to start learning. Pop was always going to teach me, but they never seemed to have any pools close to the race tracks.

She came back in a minute, and when I looked around the first thing I thought was that Dr Severance had sure been telling the truth when he said her folks was rich. Her bathing suit was made out of diamonds.

Of course, there wasn't much of it, just a string around her middle and a three-cornered patch in front, but it was all just solid diamonds. It must of cost a fortune. I wondered if it was comfortable to wear.

And then I saw the vine, the one there was such a hullaballoo about in the papers later on. It had little blue leaves, and it wound around her off bosom like a path going up a hill, and right in the centre there was this little rosebud. It was the prettiest thing I ever saw.

She stopped, all of a sudden, when she noticed how I was looking, and her eyes snapped. 'Hey,' she says, 'what goes on here? Are you a midget, or something? How old are you, kid?'

'Seven,' I says.

'Good God, what a family,' she says. 'Not even eight yet—'

Then she glanced down and saw I was looking at the vine, and she started to laugh. 'Oh,' she says. 'You had me worried there for a minute.'

'It sure is nice,' I said. 'I wish I had one.'

'Well, I wish you had this one,' she says.

'Why?' I asked.

'Well,' she says, 'I guess I developed kind of uneven when I was a kid. I had the place to put it before I had sense enough not to put it there.'

I didn't know what she was talking about, but it didn't seem to make any difference anyhow because I just figured then that all the women had vines, and that if you had one that nice it was all to the good. So we waded out in the water, kind of slow to see how deep it was. She'd had to pin her hair up on top of her head with bobby pins to keep it from getting wet because she didn't have a swimming cap.

She swam across the lake and back while I watched, so I could see how your arms and legs was supposed to go. Then she stood up and held me flat out in the water while I practised.

I began to get the hang of it in a little while and could go for two or three feet before I went under when she turned me loose.

'The main thing is, don't be afraid of water,' she says. 'It can't hurt you, so don't fight it.'

She swam across and back once more just for fun, and then we got out because it was beginning to be dusk out in the trees. Her hair had got wet on the ends in a few places, so she took a cigarette out of her handbag and we sat down on a log while she shook it out to let it dry. It was inky black, wet like that, and touching the skin on her shoulders and neck, it sure looked nice.

'By golly, you're swell,' I said. 'Teaching me to swim, and all. Can we go in every day?'

'Sure,' she says. 'Why not? I think it'll be fun.'

'I hope you'll like it here,' I said. 'Anyway, it ought to be nice and restful for you after New Orleans. All that stuff must have been pretty tiring.'

'Well,' she says, 'it was a pretty rough grind.'

When we got back to the trailer it was growing dark, and Pop and Uncle Sagamore had left. I went on down to the house, and they was in the kitchen with the lamp lit, getting supper. Uncle Sagamore was slicing the baloney and Pop was frying it.

I got some slices to feed Sig Freed, and Pop asked me if we had gone swimming. I says yes, and told them about Miss Harrington's diamond bathing suit. Him and Uncle Sagamore looked at each other, and Uncle Sagamore slipped and cut his hand with the baloney knife.

'Well, imagine that,' Pop says.

'I just did,' Uncle Sagamore says, and went off to bandage his hand.

When he came back Pop had finished frying the baloney, and they put it on the table. Uncle Finley came stalking out of his room, the one that connected with the kitchen, and sat down at the table without looking to the left or right.

He picked up a knife in one hand and a fork in the other and held them sticking straight up with his fists on the table, and says, furious like, 'Who was that there shameless hussy paradin' her naked legs around here this evenin'? Is she a-goin' to stay here?'

Uncle Sagamore grinned at Pop and says, real loud, 'Why, that ain't no way to talk about a pore gal that's in bad health, Finley.'

'Well, either she goes, or I do,' Uncle Finley says, banging the table with his fist. 'I ain't goin' to live in no place where there's sinful people like that a-wavin' theirselves around in defiance of the word of the Lord.'

Uncle Sagamore shook his head, real sad. 'Well sir, you're sure givin' us a awful hard choice, Finley. But we'll miss you. By Ned, we sure will.'

Pop asked Uncle Sagamore, not loud enough for Uncle Finley to hear, 'Do you reckon he'll really go?'

Uncle Sagamore shook his head. 'No. You don't rightly understand fellers like Finley. They figure it's their duty to stay real close to that sinful stuff and keep watchin' it, so they can stay worked up about it.'

'Yeah, I reckon that's right,' Pop says.

'Sure,' Uncle Sagamore says. 'Don't you worry. The Devil

ain't goin' to run Finley off the place by shakin' some woman's pink behind at him. He ain't no coward.'

We all sat down at the table. Uncle Finley leaned his head down and started saying grace. While he was talking, Uncle Sagamore reached over and speared about eight slices of baloney and started eating.

'Sure is nice to have some real grub for a change,' he says, 'after that goddam garden sass Bessie's always cookin' up.'

After supper me and Pop got our bedrolls out of the trailer and made 'em up on the porch. Ours wasn't a big house trailer like Dr Severance's; it was just big enough to hold the printing press and paper and our camping gear, and we always had to sleep outside. There wasn't any windows in it, either, because a lot of times we was set up pretty close to the track when we was printing the throw-away sheets, the advertising ones we ran off as soon as we'd got the results of the first six races.

We laid down and Sig Freed curled up on my blankets with me. Pop lit a cigar and I could see the end of it glowing red in the dark. Some kind of birds was yakking it up out over the river bottom, *six-furlongs-in-one-ELEVEN*, *six-furlongs-in-one-ELEVEN* over and over.

'This is sure a nice place,' I says. 'I like it here.'

'Well, that's fine,' Pop says. 'I reckon we'll stay until Fairgrounds opens in November. And looks like we might be able to build up our bankroll a little, what with gettin' a commission on Dr Severance's rent and me helpin' Sagamore a little with the tannery business.'

'Well, I sure hope he don't bring those tubs back up here,' I says.

'Oh, you get used to that and don't mind it a bit,' he says. 'As a matter of fact, according to Sagamore's formula they're goin' to be ready for a little more sun exposure about day after tomorrow.'

'Where does he sell the leather?' I asked.

'Well,' Pop says, 'he ain't exactly had any to sell yet. The first batch didn't turn out so well. It all come apart in the tubs.'

We didn't say anything for a little while, and then I remembered about all that sugar Uncle Sagamore had bought.

'What do you suppose he's going to do with that much?' I asked Pop. 'And why did he tell the sheriff he'd bought it for me?'

'Oh,' Pop says. He took another puff on the cigar and it

glowed. 'Well, it's like this, Sagamore told him that so he wouldn't have to say what it really was. He's kind of proud, and he don't like to talk to outsiders about infirmities in the family. You see, your Aunt Bessie's got the sugar diabetes, and the doctor's put her on this diet where she has to eat six pounds of sugar a day. But I wouldn't say nothing about it to anybody. They don't like it spread around.'

'Oh, I won't say nothing,' I says.

I thought it sure seemed like a place, though, for people having things wrong with 'em. Dr Severance had the heart twinge and the sheriff had the high blood pressure and Miss Harrington had the anaemia and there was the typhoid going around and now Aunt Bessie had the sugar diabetes. I hoped we didn't come down with anything like that ourselves.

The next day was really fun. I found a cane pole behind the house that had a line and hook on it and a snuff-bottle cork for a bobber, so I dug some worms and me and Sig Freed went fishing. And the funny part of it was there was real fish in the lake. I caught four. Uncle Sagamore said they was red perch, and Pop fried 'em for me for supper in the baloney grease. They was sure good.

Right after noon I wanted to go swimming, but when I went up to the trailer Miss Harrington was lying stretched out in a long canvas chair having a drink and said we couldn't go until just about sundown. Dr Severance was lying in another chair having a drink too and he says to her, 'Hey, what's with all this swimming, anyway? Don't tell me I'm being back-doored by a kid that ain't even old enough to start smoking cornsilk.'

And she says, 'Oh, shut up, can't you think about anything else for at least five minutes?'

He says, 'Well, there's gratitude for you. I save your goddam life for you, and now I got to move a seven-year-old kid out of the way every time I want to collect a little on account.'

Then she says, 'Gratitude? Believe me, buster, the next time anybody says we're going up in the country and lay around for a while, I'll know what he means.'

They kept on talking like they'd already forgot I was there, so I went back and waded around in the shallow edge of the lake just below where Uncle Finley was working on his boat, and tried to catch crawfish. The water was only about waist deep and I could see lots of 'em on the bottom but I never could catch any.

They scooted backward too fast.

Uncle Sagamore and Pop just sat around in the shade all day and talked and had a drink out of the glass jar now and then. I remembered Uncle Sagamore telling the sheriff how he had to work eighteen hours a day to pay his taxes, and I asked Pop that night if he was on vacation. Pop said it was kind of a slack season on farms right now, and that things usually picked up a little later on in the year. . . .

About sundown Miss Harrington went up to the point with me and we had another swimming lesson. She had a shower cap with her this time so her hair wouldn't get wet, and she could put her face down in the water and really swim. A crawl, she called it.

I got a little better, too. I could go six or eight feet before I went under. She said I was trying too hard to keep my face out of the water, though, and that was making me sink.

The next morning bright and early Uncle Sagamore and Pop took the truck and went down in the woods back of the cornfield and brought the tubs up to the house. The smell was even worse than it had been before. They set 'em right in the same place, along the side of the house next to the well. There wasn't much breeze, either, to blow it away.

Well, they stayed there for nearly a week, night and day, but like Pop said after a while you got used to it and didn't mind. I asked him why they didn't take 'em away at night, because there wasn't any sun then anyhow, but he says it was too much trouble to carry 'em back and forth.

About the fifth or sixth day they was there I'd got so used to the odour I could even go up to the tubs without it knocking me down, so I went over to see how the leather was coming along. I got a stick and lifted one of the cowhides up, and doggone if the stick didn't just poke right through it. It was coming apart in the tubs just like the first batch had.

I went right away to call Pop and Uncle Sagamore to tell 'em about it, but I couldn't find 'em. They'd been setting in the shade of the chinaberry tree in the back yard just a few minutes ago, having a drink out of the glass jar, but now they was gone.

I looked all around, and called, and went through the house, but I couldn't find 'em. So I walked down to the barn, and they wasn't there either, but when I went back to the house again they was setting right there under the chinaberry tree where they'd been in the first place.

When I told 'em about the leather coming apart Uncle Sagamore kind of frowned and they came around and looked theirselves. Uncle Sagamore took the stick and poked at one of the hides, and sure enough it just went right through.

He straightened up and sailed out some tobacco juice and scratched his head. 'Well sir, by golly, she sure is,' he says. 'What you reckon we're doin' that's wrong, Sam?'

Pop scratched his head too. 'Well, I just don't rightly know,' he says. 'But it sure don't look right. Leather hadn't ought to be that tender.'

'I done everything just like the bulletin says, the one I got from the gov'ment,' Uncle Sagamore says. 'I followed it real careful this time so's there couldn't be no chance for a mistake. What you reckon we ort to do?'

Pop studied for a minute. 'Only one thing we can do,' he says. 'We got to let her run full course. Ain't no sense startin' another new batch now, because she'll probably wind up just like this. We got to let her simmer right out to the end, and then when she's all finished we'll send a little bit of it to the gov'ment and ask 'em to take a look at it and tell us what we done wrong.'

'Well sir, that's the way I got her figured too,' Uncle Sagamore says, nodding his head. 'Them fellers in the gov'ment can't tell nothin' about it less'n we follow the instructions right out to the end. So we'll just let her ride. Only take about another month and a half.'

'Why, in a month and a half it probably won't be nothing but soup,' I says.

'Well, ain't nothing we can do about that,' Uncle Sagamore says. 'Just have to send 'em some of the soup, then. Instructions is instructions, and if you don't do what they say the gov'ment can't tell you nothing.'

'But look at all the time that's wasted,' I says.

Uncle Sagamore shifted his tobacco over. 'Well, hell,' he says, 'what's time to a dead cowhide, or the gov'ment?'

So they decided to do it that way. It seemed to me like we wasn't going to make much money out of the tannery if another month and a half had to go by before they started a new batch and they already knew this one was ruined, but there wasn't no use arguing with Pop and Uncle Sagamore.

I was having too much fun to worry about it, anyway. I went fishing nearly every morning, and late in the evening Miss Harrington would give me another swimming lesson. In between times, in the afternoon when she wouldn't go in, I'd practise in the shallow water at this end of the lake, just below where Uncle Finley was building his boat. And that's where the funny thing happened, the one I couldn't figure out at all.

I reckon it was the next day after we discovered the leather was ruined. It was right after noon. Sig Freed was sitting on the bank watching me, because he didn't like water, and I was wading around and practising swimming not too far from the bank, where it was about waist-deep. And all of a sudden I hit a warm place in the water.

The lake itself wasn't real cold, of course. Just kind of cool and nice, about right to swim in, but I could sure tell the difference when I hit this warm spot. It wasn't very big. I moved a couple of feet and I was out of it. I thought maybe I'd just imagined it, so I felt around and by golly I hit it again. It wasn't hot; just warm, like bath water. It was kind of spooky, and what made it so funny was that I'd been swimming and wading around here in this very spot for nearly a week and it hadn't been here before.

It just didn't make sense, any way you looked at it. It couldn't be the sun that was causing it, because the sun was shining on the whole lake. And if it was a warm spring bubbling out of the ground, why hadn't it been here those other days? I swam all around to see if I could find another one like it, but it didn't happen anywhere else. But every time I'd come back, it was still there.

After a while I got out and put my clothes on and went up to the house to ask Uncle Sagamore and Pop about it. They might have some idea why there'd be one little warm spot in a cool lake. But they wasn't there. It seemed to me like they had the funniest habit of just disappearing so you couldn't find 'em anywhere. I looked all around and waited, but they never did come back, so I dug some worms and went fishing, figuring I could ask 'em that night at supper.

But that was the day the rabbit hunters came, and there was so much happened then I forgot all about it.

It was about an hour before sundown when I went up to the trailer to see if Miss Harrington was ready to go swimming.

Dr Severance was lying in one of the chairs with a drink in his hand.

He looked at me and turned his head towards the door of the trailer, and says, 'Hey, here's Weismuller.'

Miss Harrington came out. She was wearing the candy-striped romper outfit again, and had her purse. 'Hello, Billy,' she says.

'Kid, you really slay 'em,' Dr Severance says. 'You must be a heavy spender. Or is it your breast stroke?'

'Oh, shut up,' Miss Harrington told him.

We started off through the trees, headed for the point up the lake. We'd gone maybe a couple of hundred yards and was walking along a trail where the bushes was pretty thick, with me going ahead and Miss Harrington coming behind because she was afraid of snakes, when all of a sudden I came around a bush and into a little open place, and there was a man in it.

He was just easing along real slow, looking all around through the trees, and when he saw me he jerked his head around and stared at me with his eyes real hard. He was wearing a Panama hat and a double-breasted suit, and he had a tommy gun in his hands, the kind they carry in comic books.

'Hey, punk, where'd you come from?' he asked.

'From Uncle Sagamore's,' I says. 'What you doing?'

'Huntin' rabbits,' he says. 'You seen any around?'

'Not today,' I says, but he wasn't paying any attention. He had turned and was looking up the hill. I looked too, and that's when I saw the other one. He was about fifty yards away, and was dressed just like this one, and he had a tommy gun too. He motioned with his arm, and jerked his head.

'Shhh. I think he sees one,' the first man said. He turned and slipped up that way, and they went out of sight into some more trees.

'Don't make any fuss,' I says over my shoulder to Miss Harrington. 'They're going to sneak up on a rabbit.'

She didn't say anything.

I looked around, and by golly she was gone. I didn't see her anywhere. It was funny. She'd been there a minute ago, right behind me.

'Hey, Miss Harrington,' I says, sort of low so I wouldn't scare the rabbit away.

She didn't answer. She just wasn't anywhere around. I knew she couldn't have gone on ahead, because I was standing in the trail. So I figured she must have forgot something, maybe her bathing suit, and had gone back after it. So I started back, thinking I would meet her along the trail. But when I got clear back to the trailer I still hadn't seen a sign of her. It sure was peculiar, I thought.

Dr Severance was still lying in a canvas chair with his drink. He looked at me, and says, 'Well, it's the champ. Where's Miss Harrington?'

'That's just it,' I says. 'I thought she came back here. I lost her on the trail.'

'Lost her?' he asked. 'How?'

'Well,' I says, 'I thought she was right behind me when I was talking to the rabbit hunter.'

He barked at me. 'Rabbit hunter? Where? And what did he look like?'

'Down the trail there,' I says. 'A couple of hundred yards. He was a big man with a scar on his face, and he was wearing a Panama hat and had a tommy gun.'

He came up out of the chair and threw the drink away from him all at one time, and his right hand shot inside his coat. I had to jump back real fast or he'd of run right over me. By the time I could turn around he was twenty yards down the trail.

I started to follow him, because I was still worried about what had become of Miss Harrington, but just then I saw Pop and Uncle Sagamore coming up towards the trailer.

'Where'd he go in such a hurry?' Pop asked.

I told them about Miss Harrington disappearing and about the rabbit hunters. They looked at each other.

'Well sir, is that a fact?' Uncle Sagamore says. 'Two rabbit hunters with machine-guns. It's sure lucky you got a month's rent in advance, Sam.'

'But we got to look for Miss Harrington,' I says, or started to say when Pop motioned for me to be quiet.

It seemed like they was listening for something. They just stood real still and whenever I'd start to open my mouth one or the other would shake his head at me.

Then, all of a sudden, there was two shots down the trail, just two shots real close together and then it was all quiet again. Pop and Uncle Sagamore looked at each other, and started to walk slow down that way. I started to follow them, but Pop shook his head.

'You'd better go back to the house,' he says.

'But Miss Harrington—' I says. I felt like crying, I was so worried something had happened to her. Maybe she'd fell and hurt herself.

'Never mind Miss Harrington,' Pop says. 'You go on to the house.'

They was crazy if they thought I was going back to the house when I didn't know what had become of her. So the minute they was out of sight in the trees I cut downhill and started running through the brush just below the trail. In a minute I was ahead of them. I turned to the left and got back on the trail and went running along to the place where I'd seen her last. But before I got there I happened to look uphill, and there she was, standing in a little open place in the trees. Dr Severance was with her. He was looking down at something on the ground.

I was relieved to see she was all right. I cut off the trail and ran up that way. But just before I got there he waved his hand at her and I heard him say, 'Go on back to the trailer. I'll take care of these yokels.'

She left and started walking away through the trees, and I turned and was going to run over that way to her but just then I saw Pop and Uncle Sagamore coming. If they saw me here Pop would give me a tanning for sure for not minding him. I looked around real fast, trying to see if I could get away by running in the other direction and then circling back, but there wasn't much chance. There was some thick bushes just to one side of where Dr Severance was, though, so I dived into them and hid.

Now that I knew she was all right I wasn't worried any more, so I began to be curious about what Dr Severance was doing. I parted the leaves a little where I was lying, and I could see him. He was only about ten feet away, still looking down at something lying at his feet.

There was a log in the way so I couldn't make out what it was at first, but then I saw a pair of legs in grey pants sticking out a little beyond the end of it, with the toes of the shoes pointing up in the air, and I realised what it was. It was one of those rabbit hunters. Then I saw the butt of the tommy gun, lying on the ground next to him.

And just then Dr Severance walked over a little to his right and looked down at something else, that was behind a bush. I stared over that way, and doggone if there wasn't another pair of legs sticking out from behind it too. And another tommy gun. It was the other rabbit hunter.

It sure looked like there'd been a bad accident.

Eight

Just then Pop and Uncle Sagamore walked up.

Dr Severance turned around and saw them. He took out his handkerchief and mopped his face, and shook his head kind of slow, like it was all too much for him. He sat down on the log where the first rabbit hunter was and let out a long, shaky breath.

'Gentlemen,' he says, 'it was awful. Just simply awful.'

'What happened?' Pop asked.

Dr Severance mopped his face with the handkerchief again and pointed at the rabbit hunters one at a time, with his face turned away like he didn't want to look at them. 'Dead,' he says, real said. 'They're both dead. And all on account of one crummy little rabbit.'

'Well sir, that's a shame,' Uncle Sagamore says. 'Just how did it happen?'

'Well,' Dr Severance says, taking a deep breath and beginning to get a-hold of hisself a little, 'I was standing down there by the trail when I saw these two men walking by up here looking for rabbits. I was just about to call out and ask 'em if they'd had any luck, when all of a sudden this little brown rabbit popped out of a bush right between 'em. It started to run off, but then for some reason it changed its mind and doubled back, right square between the two of 'em just as they both raised their guns and shot. It was the most terrible thing I ever saw in my life. They just killed each other deader than hell.'

Uncle Sagamore bent down and looked at the first rabbit hunter. He walked over to the other one and rolled him over a little and looked at him too. Then he came back and hunkered down and took out his plug of tobacco. He wiped it on the leg of his overalls, and bit off a big chew, and shook his head.

'Yes sir, by golly,' he says, 'it sure must of been a heart-rendin' thing to see. Pore fellers just shot each other right in the back.'

Dr Severance nodded. 'That's right. That was what made it so terrible. You felt so sorry for 'em, because they knew it was coming and there wasn't a thing in the world they could do about it. They both saw what they'd done by the time they pulled the triggers. They turned around and tried to duck, but it was too late.'

Uncle Sagamore sailed out some tobacco juice and wiped his

mouth with the back of his hand. 'Well sir,' he says, 'that there's the tragic thing about all these city fellers wanderin' around in the woods a-huntin'. They're helpless. They're dangerous to theirselves, and that's a fact, because they don't know how to handle guns.'

He stopped and looked at Dr Severance, and then he says, 'But don't get me wrong. I don't mean they're all like that. Once in a while you run across one that's just hell on wheels with a gun, and I wouldn't want you to think I was lumpin' all city fellers together that way. No offence, mind you.'

'No,' Dr Severance says. 'No. Of course not.'

'But that ain't neither here nor there,' Uncle Sagamore went on. 'I reckon what we got to do now is notify the shurf and explain to him how these pore fellers killed theirselves, and ask him to haul 'em away, it bein' warm weather and all.'

Dr Severance nodded. 'Sure. I guess that's the least we can do.'

Then all of a sudden he stopped and rubbed his chin with his hand, his face screwed up kind of thoughtful. 'Hmmmmm,' he says. 'Gentlemen, I just remembered something.'

He reached back and got his wallet out of his hip pocket and held it in his lap while he started taking stuff out of it like he was looking for something. I watched him through the leaves, trying to figure out what he was doing. He slid out a thick bundle of money that would of choked a horse, and just dropped it across his legs as careless as if it'd been a bunch of old socks, while he went on poking around in the wallet.

Pop and Uncle Sagamore looked at all the bills.

'What is it you're looking for?' Pop asked.

'Oh,' Dr Severance says. 'Why, my copy of the game laws.' He held the empty wallet up, spreading it open so he could look inside. 'I could have sworn I had it with me, but I must have left it in my other suit.'

'The game laws?' Uncle Sagamore asked.

'That's right,' Dr Severance says, putting the stuff back in the wallet, the money last. He had to shuffle it around a little to get it all packed in. 'However, it don't matter that I haven't got it with me. I remember the laws perfectly, because I just looked at them yesterday. And, gentlemen, do you know what?'

'What's that?' Uncle Sagamore asked.

'Mind you,' Dr Severance says, 'I wouldn't say this if I didn't know I was right. But the rabbit season closed two weeks ago.'

'No!' Uncle Sagamore says, his mouth falling open. 'Is that a fact?' He thought for a minute, and then he clapped his hands together, and says, 'Yes, by hell, I believe you're right. I recollect now, I looked it up just the other day myself.'

'Why,' Pop says, looking at the two rabbit hunters, 'they ought to of been ashamed of theirselves, a-huntin' rabbits out of season that way. They're no better than common criminals.'

'It's people like that,' Uncle Sagamore says, 'that destroy the natural resources of a country. It's just disheartenin', that's what it is. Out here, sneakin' around and breakin' the laws behind people's backs.'

Dr Severance nodded. 'That's right. And as for me, I wouldn't hardly have the guts to go bothering a poor overworked sheriff with 'em. He's got enough on his mind now, protecting the citizens, and looking for live criminals.'

'Why, sure,' Uncle Sagamore says. 'That's what makes taxes so damn high now, everybody unloadin' his troubles on the gov'ment and runnin' to the shurf with every two-bit thing that comes up. People just ain't got no consideration.'

'Now, that's it, exactly,' Dr Severance says. 'You've put your finger right on it. What if we are taxpayers? Why should we start throwing our weight around, and raise a big stink and demand that the sheriff drop everything he's doing just to come running out here because a couple of criminals has had an accident while they was deliberately trying to kill a poor rabbit out of season? Especially after I caught 'em right in the act. It makes me real happy to know I've met up with a couple of public-spirited men that see it the same way I do.'

Uncle Sagamore spat again and wiped his mouth with the back of his hand. 'Well sir,' he says, 'it's real nice of you to say that. Now, just what did you have in mind?'

'Why,' Dr Severance says, 'I was thinking, since there's plenty of vacant land back in here in the trees, why don't we just give 'em a private burial and forget the whole shameful thing?'

Uncle Sagamore nodded. 'Why, that's a fine idea. Don't know why I didn't think of it myself.' Then he stopped and thought about it again, and looked kind of doubtful. 'Of course,' he went on, 'a thing like that might run into quite a little work, what with the diggin' and all, and I just don't rightly see how me and Sam could spare the time away from the crop, workin' practically night and day like we are.'

'Oh, I'd be glad to bear the expense of it,' Dr Severance says. 'I feel kind of responsible, since I was the one discovered 'em.

What do you say to maybe a hundred dollars?'

'Fine,' Uncle Sagamore says. 'Fine.'

But then he stopped, like he'd just thought of something and his face looked sad. He shook his head. 'Well sir,' he went on, 'it's a shame. A downright shame. I thought there for a minute we had the answer, but we just can't do it.'

'Can't? Why not?' Dr Severance asked.

'Well, it's kind of a personal matter,' Uncle Sagamore says, like he didn't want to talk about it. 'But you see, this here land's been in my family quite a spell. Matter of fact, my pappy and grandpappy's both buried on it. And I – well, I know it may sound kind of silly, but to be truthful I'm afraid it might get to weighin' on my mind later on, thinkin' of them being buried in the same ground with a couple of low-down men that'd do a thing like shootin' a rabbit out of season.'

'Yes, that's right,' Dr Severance says. 'It sure might, at that.' Then his face brightened up. 'But say, just for the sake of argument, that it did start bothering your conscience later on. What do you figure it would cost to have your folks moved to a regular cemetery?'

'Why,' Uncle Sagamore says, 'I expect about five hundred dollars.'

'Well, that sounds like a reasonable figure,' Dr Severance says. He counted some bills out of his wallet and handed them to Uncle Sagamore. 'Six hundred altogether.'

He sure carried a lot of money around with him. It didn't hardly make a dent on what was in the wallet. I could see that even from where I was. Pop and Uncle Sagamore looked at what was left, and then at each other.

'Well, I reckon that takes care of everything,' Uncle Sagamore says. He started to get up. Then he stopped all of a sudden, looking kind of thoughtful, and hunkered down again. 'Well sir, by golly,' he says, 'do you know what we plumb forgot?'

Dr Severance looked at him real sharp. 'Now what?'

'The sermon,' Uncle Sagamore says. 'Ain't no man deserves to be buried without preachin', no matter what he done. We just naturally couldn't send these two sinners to their last restin' place without a minister. Couldn't even think of it.'

'Minister?' Dr Severance says. 'How the hell are we going to have a minister at a private funeral like this?'

'Well sir,' Uncle Sagamore says. 'It's easy. Seems like the luck is right with us all the way. It just happens my brother Sam here is a ordained minister of the gospel, and I know we could get him to say a few words.'

'Hmmmm,' Dr Severance says. 'That is a piece of luck, ain't it? And how much does his fee run?'

'Well,' Uncle Sagamore says, 'as a usual thing, a hundred dollars a head.'

'That sounds like a nice round figure,' Dr Severance says, reaching for his wallet again.

'However, in this case,' Uncle Sagamore went on, 'seein' as how these men died with all that sin on 'em, right in the committin' of a crime, so to speak, Brother Sam might have to throw in a few extra flourishes to get 'em over the hump. Still and all, though, I reckon that two hundred dollars a head ought to just about cover it.'

Dr Severance counted out some more money and handed it to him. 'You boys are wasting your time farming,' he says. 'You got too much talent to be rusting away out here in the sticks.'

'Well sir, it's downright nice of you to say so,' Uncle Sagamore says. He stood up. 'Well, I reckon me an' Brother Sam can take care of all the arrangements. You figure on comin' to the services?'

Dr Severance shook his head. 'I'd sure like to, but I thought I'd drive back down the road and see if these boys didn't leave a car somewhere.'

Uncle Sagamore nodded. 'That's a right smart idea. Kind of drive it back to town, or somewhere, an' make it easier for their families to find it.'

'That's about what I had in mind,' Dr Severance says. He went off up the trail.

Pop was still sitting on the log, puffing on his cigar. As soon as Dr Severance had went out of sight, he says to Uncle Sagamore, 'If these is the same bunch of rabbit hunters I seen in town, there was three of 'em.'

Uncle Sagamore pursed up his lips like he was going to sail out some tobacco juice. 'Three?' he says.

'Reckon we ort to tell him?' Pop asked.

'Ain't no call for us to go stickin' our nose in things that don't concern us, Sam,' Uncle Sagamore says. 'If he don't find no car up there, he's going to know it hisself.'

'But supposin' he does find the car? One of these might have the keys.'

'Well it still ain't none of our business, Sam. We wouldn't want to cause him no worry, would we? A man that pays his bills like that and minds his own business? If he got to frettin' about what happened to the other one, he might even leave. We wouldn't want that to happen, would we?'

He looked at the wad of money he was still holding in his hand, and Pop looked at it. Uncle Sagamore shoved it in his pocket.

'I reckon you're right,' Pop says. 'Sure wouldn't want to drive away a good customer with triflin' little worries like that. He looks like a dude that could take care of hisself, anyway.'

'Sure,' Uncle Sagamore says. 'Ain't no call for us to put in our oar, Sam. Way I look at it, he want any advice from us he'd of asked us. An' he said them fellers was just huntin' rabbits, didn't he?'

'Sure,' Pop says. He got up off the log. 'Well, I reckon I ort to get a couple of shovels.'

Uncle Sagamore shook his head. 'Ain't no use makin' hard work out of a simple job like this. We'll just bring the truck in here after dark, and hold the services over at the old Hawkins place. Ain't nobody lived in that tenant house for five years, an' the well's dry and about to cave in, anyway.'

They started back towards the house, and as soon as they was out of sight I skinned out too, circling up the side of the hill to pass them before they got home. I come out of the trees near the trailer, and Dr Severance and Miss Harrington was just getting in their car.

I waved at her. I was just about to ask her if she still wanted to go swimming, and then I remembered that what with the accident to the two rabbit hunters likely everybody was feeling pretty bad and she wouldn't want to.

She waved back, but she looked kind of pale. Dr Severance didn't say anything. He just shot the car ahead with the tyres spinning. He looked real mad.

I went on over to the house and played with Sig Freed on the front porch, and in a few minutes Pop and Uncle Sagamore come along. Of course I didn't let on I'd been down there.

'Miss Harrington's all right,' I says to Pop.

'Well, that's good,' he says.

'I seen her drive off in the car with Dr Severance.'

Pop and Uncle Sagamore looked at each other, and Pop took another cigar out and lit it. 'I been meaning to tell you,' he says, 'I think you better quit hangin' around so much with Miss Harrington. That anaemia might be catching.'

'Aw, Pop,' I says. 'I like her. And besides, she's teaching me how to swim.'

'Well, you just mind what I tell you,' Pop tells him. Him and Uncle Sagamore went on around the house. I got to thinking about it and in a few minutes I went around to the back yard myself to ask him if it wasn't all right to go swimming with her now that she didn't have to hold me up any more. I couldn't catch the anaemia if she wasn't touching me, could I? But they wasn't back there. I went down to the barn, but they wasn't down there either.

Well, I thought, maybe they went off in the woods beyond the cornfield for something. Then I remembered about that warm place in the lake that I was going to ask Uncle Sagamore about, so I went down there and took my clothes off and waded out to look for it again. And, by golly, *it* was gone too. I just couldn't find it anywhere. I'd marked right where it was, too. You lined up the back end of Finley's ark with the corner of the front porch and waded out about eight steps till the water was up to your hips and there it was. Only it wasn't. Now the water was just the same there as it was anywhere else. It sure was funny. I went out on the bank and thought about it while I waited for myself to dry off, but it just didn't make any sense at all. Only thing it could be, I thought, is a kind of warm spring that don't run all the time.

It was close on to sundown, and I went back up to the house. Pop and Uncle Sagamore had come back from wherever they had went. Pop was slicing baloney and Uncle Sagamore was frying it. They was both kind of quiet and it didn't look like they would take much to the idea of answering questions, so I didn't ask any.

After supper Pop said they was going to bring up the truck and haul the tubs back down in the woods; the leather had had enough sun for a few days. He said they might go in to town afterwards, so not to wait up.

I got scared lying on the front porch in the dark, thinking about the accident the rabbit hunters had, but I could hear Uncle Finley snoring away in the back bedroom so it wasn't too lonesome.

When I woke up in the morning the sun was shining in my face and I could see it was going to be another fine day for fishing. Sig Freed was licking my face and I could hear Pop and Uncle Sagamore frying the baloney for breakfast back in the kitchen. I got up and raced Sig Freed down to the lake to wash up. Just as I was coming in the kitchen door I heard Uncle Sagamore say to Pop,

'Reckon he must of found it, all right, and drove it clear out of the state. Heard him come in about four this morning.'

Then they seen me, and looked at each other. Uncle Sagamore started talking about the leather business.

'Sure can't figure it out,' he says, throwing some more slices of baloney in the hot grease. 'Couldn't of followed them gov'ment instructions no closer'n I did, and still she's sure as hell turnin' into soup. You reckon we just ain't got the right kind of climate up here to make leather, Sam?'

'Well, it could be,' Pop says. 'Or it might be the water. Ain't nothing we can do, though, but just keep tryin'. Can't give up.'

After breakfast I took Sig Freed and went up by the trailer. The doctor and Miss Harrington wasn't up, so I went fishing. It was a nice day and I caught some more perch. Along in the afternoon I saw Miss Harrington and the doctor sitting in their chairs in front of the trailer, but when I went up there she said she didn't want to go swimming today.

It was three days before she would go again. Then Pop give me a licking when he found out about it.

'I told you to stay away from Miss Harrington,' he says. 'She's not a well girl, and you might catch her anaemia.'

It was another ten days before we got to go in again, and then I had to sneak off. And that was the day all hell busted loose.

But first there was this hullaballoo with the sheriff's men that got everybody excited.

Nine

It started out just like any other day. It was time to bring the leather out of the woods for a little more sun, so Pop and Uncle Sagamore took the truck and hauled the tubs up to the house just after breakfast. The stuff was all coming to pieces now and it smelled worse than ever. There wasn't any breeze, either, to blow it away, so it just hung around the house something awful. It was bubbling a little, and had a thick scum, kind of brown and green, on it.

It made my eyes water, so I went down to watch Uncle Finley to get away from it. He had run clear out of boards, so he was busy pulling 'em off one place and nailin 'em on in another, just kind of patching, as Uncle Sagamore called it.

He kept muttering to hisself and wouldn't talk, so after a while I went up towards the trailer to see what Miss Harrington was doing. She and the doctor was sitting in the canvas chairs out in front, listening to the little radio on the table. It was giving the morning news. He just grunted at me, but she went inside and got me a coke.

She was wearing a white romper suit this time, and she sure looked nice. 'Do you want to go swimming this evening, Billy?' she asked me.

'I'd sure love to,' I says. 'But Pop might give me another licking.'

'Tell him to go fry an ice cube,' she says. 'I'll tell you what. You meet me over there about five o'clock, and we'll go in anyway.'

Dr Severance gave her a dirty look and switched off the radio. 'You stay around the trailer, like I told you. We're not out of the woods yet.'

'Stop being such a square,' she says. 'It's been ten days.'

Just then I looked down the hill towards the house and saw Pop lying under the back end of the car like he was working on it. 'I'll see you at five o'clock,' I said to Miss Harrington, and started down that way with Sig Freed to see what he was doing.

Just before I got there he straightened up, and I saw he had a tin can in his hand. It looked to me like he must have been draining some gasoline out of the tank. He went on around the corner of the house, and then I saw Uncle Sagamore coming up from the barn carrying four glass jars.

I wondered what they was going to put gasoline in fruit jars for, and why they needed four big ones like that for just one little can full. I had to grab my nose when I got down close to the tubs, but I went on and looked around the corner of the house. It was funny what they was doing.

There was a little table sitting in the back yard in the shade of the chinaberry tree. Uncle Sagamore had put the four glass jars on it, and Pop was dipping a piece of white string in the can of gasoline. When it was good and wet, he took it out fast and tied it around the middle of one of the jars. Uncle Sagamore struck a match and touched it to the string. It blazed up and made a ring of fire around the jar for a minute before it went out. Then they did the same thing to the next one, with another piece of string. I watched. There didn't seem to be any sense to it. They kept on till they had done it to all four of them. Then they took off the charred strings and rubbed the jars clean with a cloth, handling them real gentle.

I walked up behind them. 'Hey, Pop,' I says, 'what you doing?'

They both whirled around, and looked at me and then at each other. 'Doing?' Pop says. 'Why, uh – we're testing these jars. Ain't that what it looks like?'

'Testing 'em?' I says. 'Why?'

Uncle Sagamore pursed up his lips and spit out some tobacco juice. 'Well sir,' he says, 'it's just like I was telling you, Sam. A boy ain't never goin' to learn nothin' less'n he asks questions. Now, how would a young boy know you don't never send nothin' to the gov'ment in jars you ain't sure of? He got any way of knowin' what would happen if one of them jars busted along the way, or after it got there? He don't know nothin' about how the gov'ment operates.'

He stopped and shifted his tobacco over into his other cheek and wiped his mouth with the back of his hand. Then he looks at me real solemn and goes on, 'Now you take if one of them jars was to happen to bust, you got the whole goddam gov'ment in a uproar. Before you know it, they're faunchin' around like a pen full of hawgs after a rattlesnake, with everybody millin' around askin' questions and trying to figure out what happened. Then somebody gets a burr under his crupper and starts a investigation, so you got all them high-priced people tied up wastin' time just because some pore old ignorant boll weevil that didn't know no better sent 'em something in a rickety fruit jar that wouldn't hold together. And that ain't all. Right in the middle of all this hullaballoo, somebody discovers the gov'ment ain't even got a regular fruit-jar testing department. So two more people start a investigation to find out how come they ain't, and four others start a investigation to find out how come the first two ain't investigated this already, and in the meantime some janitor sweeps up the busted fruit jar and throws it out, so everybody drops everything and comes chargin' in to investigate him, and the first thing you know the whole thing's like a fire in a whorehouse.'

'And that makes taxes go up,' Pop says.

'Yes, sir,' Uncle Sagamore says, 'that's exactly what it does.'

'Oh,' I says. 'Are you going to send something to the gov'ment?'

'That's right.' Uncle Sagamore nodded his head. 'Me an' Sam got to thinkin' about what you said about all the time we'd waste lettin' this leather run its course, so we figured maybe we ort to kind of hurry the thing along a little by sendin' 'em some of the juice now an' letting 'em see if maybe they could tell us what was wrong. We're goin' to have some of her analysed by the gov'ment.'

'Well,' I says, 'that seems to me like the right thing to do. Then, if they say you didn't mix the juice just right to begin with, you can start over with a new batch without having to wait all that time.' I felt real proud of myself. They'd seen I was right.

Uncle Sagamore nodded. 'That's just the way me and Sam saw it. You got a good head on you.'

'And you're going to ship her in those four jars?' I ask. 'You reckon they'll need that much?'

Uncle Sagamore pursed up his lips. 'Well, we don't rightly know just how much the gov'ment usually has to have for tests like this, so we figured to be on the safe side we'd ort to send 'em two gallons.' He stopped and looked at me. 'That strike you as about right?'

'Yeah,' I says. 'Sure. If it don't cost too much to ship it.'

'Oh, that's all right,' he says. 'We'll send her collect. Ain't no strain about that.'

Pop got a water bucket and a dipper out of the kitchen. Circling around to get upwind of the tubs, because there was a little breeze beginning to blow now, he fanned the air with his hat in front of his face while he swished back the foam and bubbles a little and began dipping some of the juice out into the bucket. When he trotted back to the chinaberry tree with the bucket full his eyes was watering and he was choking a little.

'Startin' to be a little on the ripe side,' he says.

Uncle Sagamore nodded. 'She does seem to be gettin' a little tang to her.'

Sig Freed whined and ran down towards the barn. I didn't blame him much. Pop got a strainer out of the kitchen and began filling the four jars. The strainer caught the bubbles and strips of cowhide so the tanning juice in the jars was clear.

'Got to remember to wash them utensils out before Bessie gets back,' Uncle Sagamore said. 'She gits provoked about usin' 'em for things like this.'

'Hadn't you ought to put in a couple of pieces of the leather?' I asked. 'Maybe they'll want to analyse it too.'

Uncle Sagamore shook his head. 'No. I reckon not. The solution's the only thing the gov'ment is interested in. That's what does the work an' tans the leather, an' when they find out what I done wrong when I mixed her up we'll be all set.'

He picked up one of the jars real easy and held it up to squint through it at the light.

'How is she for colour?' Pop asked.

'Real good,' Uncle Sagamore says. 'She just couldn't be better. Like a regular carr-mel job.'

I couldn't see what difference the colour made. You could see it was about like weak tea but, heck, what did the gov'ment care about that?

Uncle Sagamore slipped a rubber ring around the neck of each one of the jars and got ready to screw on the caps. 'Got to be sure we seal her good and tight,' he says.

'We got just the thing out in the trailer,' Pop says. He went through the house. In a minute he came back with a tube of clear cement. He smeared some on both sides of the rubber sealing ring and a little on the edges of the caps, and they screwed 'em down firm, holding on to the shoulders of the jars with their other hand. Pop threw what was left of the juice back in one of the tubs, and washed out the bucket. Then they washed off the outsides of the jars. You couldn't smell it now, except what was coming from the tubs themselves.

Uncle Sagamore went and got a cardboard box and packed the four jars in it real careful, stuffing wadded paper all around them so they couldn't touch each other and break. Pop took the box out and put it in the back of our car.

'You goin' to take it to the post office now?' I asked.

'Sure,' Pop says.

'Can I go, Pop?'

'Sure, I reckon so,' he says. 'Come to think of it, haven't you got a lot of old dirty clothes we ort to take to the laundry while we're goin'?'

'Yeah,' I says. 'I'll get 'em.'

I went in the trailer and found the laundry sack behind the printing press. It was full of my stuff and Pop's shorts and levis and shirts and socks and things. Some of 'em hadn't been sent to the laundry since we was at Bowie. There was a lot of 'em. Pop took the bag and put it in the back of the car, on top of the box that had the jars in it.

'Maybe they'd ride better on top of the clothes,' I says. 'Like a cushion, so there won't be no chance of 'em breaking.'

'No, they're all right,' Pop says. 'We tested them jars, didn't we?'

'Okay,' I says. I started to climb in the back. 'Are we ready to go? Where's Uncle Sagamore?'

Pop lit a cigar. 'Oh, he'll be along in a few minutes. He had to run down in the bottom to see about one of the mules.'

'Oh,' I says. 'Well, why don't we pull the car up a little so we can get away from them tubs?',

'That's a good idea,' Pop says. He moved the car up the hill about fifty yards and we sat in it while we waited for Uncle Sagamore. It was hot and sunshiny, and I could hear that bug yakking it up out in the trees. It was real nice, I thought, especially since we was out of range and couldn't smell them tubs. The country sure was a nice place, all peaceful like this, and not crowded like Pimlico and Belmont Park. I could see Dr Severance and Miss Harrington sitting in their chairs in front of the trailer listening to the radio. They waved at us. Pop looked up in that direction.

'A diamond bathing suit,' he says, more like he was talking to hisself. 'Imagine that. Where do you swim, you an' Miss Harrington?'

'We don't,' I says. 'You told me not to, don't you remember?'

'Oh. Yeah, I did, didn't I?'

He was quiet for a minute, and then he looked back up the hill again and stirred kind of restless in the seat. 'Reckon if it's made out of diamonds, it ain't a very big suit, is it?'

'No,' I said. 'Just a little three-cornered patch, sort of, and a string that goes around the middle.'

'Just one patch?'

'Yeah,' I says. 'Leaves her lots of room to swim. It ain't binding at all.'

'*Ho-ly* hell!' he says, like he was choking on the cigar smoke. 'You're sure there ain't *three* patches?'

'No. Just one. Why? Is there usually three?'

'Oh,' he says. 'I don't rightly know. Seems like I heard somewhere there was three, most generally. But I reckon it don't make no difference. You see anything of Sagamore?'

I turned and looked down past the house and across the corn-field, but I didn't see him anywhere. 'Not yet.'

'Well, he'll be along pretty soon.'

'Is something wrong with one of the mules?' I asked.

'Well, with a mule, it's kind of hard to tell when something *is* wrong with him. But he says one of 'em has been actin' kind of funny. Like something was worryin' him.'

'Oh,' I says. We waited some more. And then, when I looked down that way again, I saw a little feather of grey smoke coming up above the trees way down in the bottom.

'Say, Pop. Something's burning down there.'

He turned that way. 'Well, by golly, so it is. I reckon it ain't serious, though. Likely just an old stump or something.'

Just then there was a racket up the hill. It sounded like a car coming along the old road in a big hurry, I turned and got just a glimpse of it as it passed an opening in the trees. It didn't turn in at the wire gate, though; it just kept on going on that road that angled down towards the bottom. It was really moving.

'They was travelling a little like Booger and Otis,' I says. 'You reckon it was them?'

'Hmmmm,' Pop says. 'I don't know. Can't see why they'd be goin' down there towards the bottom.'

'Maybe they seen that smoke. Uncle Sagamore says they keep a sharp lookout for forest fires.'

Pop took a puff on his cigar. 'Reckon that might be it, at that. Well, they'll likely put her out. Ain't no cause to worry.'

He kept on looking down towards the timber, and in a minute Uncle Sagamore came out of it on the far side of the cornfield. He was walking pretty fast. He went in the back of the house, and then come on out the front just like he'd walked straight through, but when he came out he had on a pair of shoes. The shoes wasn't laced, though, and he didn't have on a shirt. He didn't believe in dressing up much to go to town. The black hair on his chest stuck up above the bib of his overalls, and it was all sweaty when he walked up to the car and got in the front seat with Pop.

Pop started the car. 'That mule all right?' he asks.

'Mule?' Uncle Sagamore asked. 'Oh. Sure. Looks in pretty good shape. He was just sulkin', I reckon.'

'That was likely it,' Pop says.

'Mules is a lot like women,' Uncle Sagamore went on. 'They get to thinkin' about some triflin' thing that happened ten, fifteen years ago, an' then they brood about it for a while and go into a sull an' won't have nothing' to do with you for weeks. An' the hell of it is you ain't got no idea at all what they're poutin' about.'

'I reckon that's right,' Pop says. He eased the car up the hill, taking it slow and easy across the bumps. Uncle Sagamore got out and opened the wire gate. We went through and he got back in. We started up the sandy road through the pines. Just before we got to the top of the hill the car stalled. It just stopped right in its tracks.

'Well,' Pop says. 'Why you reckon it did that?'

'Sure is funny.' Uncle Sagamore says. 'Mebbe you better try the starter.'

Pop ground on the starter, but nothing happened. He pulled out the choke and ground some more. It didn't start.

I looked over his shoulder. 'Hey, Pop,' I says. 'I see the trouble. Looks like the key ain't turned all the way on.'

'Of course it's turned on,' Pop says.

'But, look—'

'Damn it,' Pop barks at me. 'I tell you the key is all right.' He went on grinding on the starter, with the choke pulled all the way out.

'But, Pop—'

'Will you hush about that key?' he snaps at me. 'Look—' He took hold of the key, and sure enough it did turn a little. It hadn't been quite all the way on, just like I told him.

'Well, I'll be dad-burned,' he says.

'Well sir, the fool thing,' Uncle Sagamore says. 'Who would of thought that?'

Pop pushed on the starter again. 'Well, we'll go now.' The engine turned over, but nothing happened. It wouldn't start.

'I think you got it flooded,' I says.

'Something's sure wrong,' Pop got out. Then Uncle Sagamore opened his door and got out too. Pop raised up the hood, and they stood looking at the motor.

'Reckon there could be something wrong amongst all them wires?' Uncle Sagamore asked. 'Such a passel of 'em in there, man wouldn't never know if they was hooked up right.'

I didn't bother to get out. You could see what was wrong. He'd been turning the motor over all that time with the switch off and the choke pulled out, and he'd flooded her. As soon as it set for a few minutes it'd be all right. Funny Pop couldn't figure that out; he knew a right smart about motors as a rule. But it was all right with me. It was nice there, all sunshiny and warm, with a little breeze whispering through the tops of the pines. I just sat there with my feet on the bag of dirty clothes and wondered if we'd get back in time so I could go swimming with Miss Harrington. I sure hoped so.

Just then there was the sound of another car coming up the road behind us, coming real fast like whoever it was was in a big hurry. They threw on the brakes and slid to a stop in the ruts right behind us. I got out to see who it was. And doggone if it wasn't Booger and Otis in the sheriff car.

They got out, one on each side. They had on their white hats, pushed back on their heads kind of free-and-easy like, and their gun-belts, with the bone-handled guns hanging down on their right leg. They both had on a little short khaki jacket and a black tie, and they looked real spruce. There was a kind of grin on their faces, like they'd both thought of the same joke at the same time. Booger's gold tooth just shined.

Uncle Sagamore straightened up and looked at them, and then he grinned kind of sheepish. 'Well sir, by golly,' he says, 'if it ain't the shurf's boys, Sam. You recollect Booger and Otis, don't you?'

Pop looked at Uncle Sagamore, and Uncle Sagamore looked at Pop, both of 'em like they was uneasy about something and trying not to let on. Then Pop swallowed like he had something stuck in his throat and said, 'Why, sure I do. I'm real proud to see you boys again.'

Booger and Otis walked on around the car real slow, not saying a word. When they got in the road in front of it they just stood there with their thumbs hooked in the gun-belts. They looked at each other in a way that made you think they was going to bust out laughing any minute, but then their faces got real serious.

'Why – uh – you having a little trouble, Mr Noonan?' Booger asked, real anxious. He didn't mean Pop, though, because he was looking at Uncle Sagamore.

But before Uncle Sagamore could say anything, Otis says, 'Why, Booger, I do believe Mr Noonan's car has broke down.'

Booger looked amazed. 'Well, is that a fact?' he asked. 'Now, ain't that a embarrassing thing to happen? I mean, right at a time like this.'

Otis nodded his head real solemn. 'It sure is,' he says. 'But ain't he the lucky one we come along so we could help him?'

Uncle Sagamore pulled his right foot out of his shoe and used his big toenail to scratch his other leg with. He looked down at the ground. 'Shucks, boys,' he says. 'I don't reckon it's nothin' very serious. Likely me an' Sam can get her goin', an' we wouldn't want to put you boys out none, you bein' busy an' all. I think you can get around us all right, by just pullin' out of the ruts.'

Booger and Otis stared at each other, like they was horrified just even thinking about it. 'Go off and leave you broke down like this? Why, Mr Noonan, we wouldn't even dream of it,' Otis says. 'Good heaven, Booger, how many times you reckon the sheriff has told us? Boys, he always says, any time you can be of any help to Mr Noonan, you just pitch right in there and give him a hand. Mr Noonan's a taxpayer, Otis he tells me. I know for a fact his taxes is paid in full right up through 1937.'

Uncle Sagamore took out his big red handkerchief and mopped his face, and then rubbed it around on top of the bald spot on his head. 'Well sir, you boys make me feel real proud, talkin' like that, an' it's downright neighbourly of you to offer to help, but me an' Sam ain't in no hurry an' we'd just be mortified at causin' you any sort of trouble.'

Booger held up a hand. 'Not another word, Mr Noonan. Not – another – word. Pu-leese! What kind of men you think is in the sheriff's department, if they can't help out a fine upstandin' citizen like you when they see him in trouble?' He stopped then and looked at Otis. 'I say there, Mr Sears, you know a little something about motors, don't you?'

'Why, yes, Mr Ledbetter, a little,' Otis says.

Booger nodded. 'Well, that's fine. Now. What would you say might be causin' the trouble?'

Otis put his chin in the palm of his right hand and sort of frowed. 'Hmmmm,' he says. 'Now this here is just a guess, mind you, but offhand I'd say they's a pretty good chance it's a plugged gas line.'

'Well, is that a fact?' Booger asked. 'Now. Where would you start to look for a thing like that?'

Otis scratched his head and looked real thoughtful. 'Well, there's a number of places she might be clogged up. We might look in the trunk, or under the back seat, or in the upholstery, or even underneath, along the frame.'

'But wait a minute,' Booger interrupts him. 'Wouldn't you need a search warrant to go poking around in somebody's car like that?'

'Why, shucks, no, I wouldn't think so,' Otis says. 'Not to look for a clogged gas line.' He turned to Uncle Sagamore. 'Ain't that your opinion, Mr Noonan?'

Uncle Sagamore mopped his face again. 'Why – uh—' he says.

'Why, of course not,' Otis says. 'It'd just be silly. A neighbourly gesture like that?'

So they walked along on each side of the car. Booger come to the back door I had left open when I got out. He stuck his head in and hefted the bag of clothes.

'Well, well,' he says. 'What have we got here? Looks like a whole passel of laundry. And, by golly, here's a cardboard box under it, where you wouldn't hardly notice it if you didn't happen to be lookin' for a clogged gas line. Box just settin' there, all covered up.'

Otis came around to that side too. They looked at each other, real puzzled.

'What do you reckon is in there?' Otis asked.

Booger shook the box a little.

'Well, heavens to Betsy,' he says. 'Listen. It sort of gurgles. You reckon it's surp, or perfume, or something? Maybe it's Channel Number Five he's taking to one of his lady friends.' He thought for a minute, and then slapped his hands together. 'No. I know what it is. I bet Mr Noonan has got some spare gasoline in this here box.'

Uncle Sagamore scratched his left leg with his right toenail again.

'Why, shucks, boys,' he says. 'That there's just some of my tannery solution. I was gonna send it to the gov'ment to have it analysed.'

Booger and Otis straightened up. 'Well, what do you know about that?' they says. 'Tannery solution. Who would of thought it?'

'Sure,' Uncle Sagamore says. 'That's all it is, boys.' Then he looks down inside the hood at the motor again and points a finger and says to Pop, 'Hey, Sam, how about that there loose wire? You reckon that could be causin'—'

'Well, I'll be dad-burned,' Pop says. 'That's it, for sure. Now, why didn't I see it before?' He bent over the fender and reached in under the hood. Then he straightened up. 'Well, she'll run now.'

Uncle Sagamore patted the bald spot on his head again with the handkerchief. 'Well, we're sure obliged to you boys for stoppin' to help,' he says. 'Reckon we'll run along.'

'Oh, don't rush off, Mr Noonan,' Booger says. He winked at Otis, and they both grinned.

Otis reached into the cardboard box and brought out one of the jars of tannery juice. He held it up to the light and squinted at it.

'Hmmmm,' he says. 'Sure is a purty colour. I reckon Mr Noonan has been puttin' a little burnt sugar in his tannery solution, Booger. Gives it that aged-in-the-wood look, just like Old Grandpaw.'

Ten

They looked at each other real solemn, but you could see they was having trouble keeping their faces straight. Then Otis snickered. And then Booger snickered. They busted into a regular guffaw. Next thing, they're having to hold each other up, they're laughing so hard.

Booger wiped the tears out of his eyes. 'Tannery solution!' he says, and then doubled up and started to howl again. They both leaned against the car, just whooping. You could of heard 'em a mile.

At last they get control of theirselves again, and Booger says, 'Well, I reckon we better get going. We'll leave her right in there, so they can confiscate the car too. You get in the back seat and ride in with them, Otis, and I'll foller in the other car.'

Pop jumped up like he'd been stung. 'Hey, what are you fellers talkin' about? Confiscate the car? This is *my* car.'

Otis stared at him. 'Well, mister, you sure picked a hell of a poor time to say that.'

'Now, look, boys,' Uncle Sagamore says, 'you're makin' a big mistake. I tell you that's just tannery solution I'm sendin' to the gov'ment.'

Booger just shook his head. He was too weak to laugh any more. 'Wait till the sheriff hears that one,' he says. 'Boy, I can hardly wait to see his face when we drive up. All the years he's been tryin'—'

It seemed to me like the joke had gone far enough, whatever it was. I couldn't figure why they wouldn't believe Uncle Sagamore, but somebody ought to straighten 'em out. 'But, look, Mr

Booger,' I says, 'it *is* tannery juice.'

Pop and Uncle Sagamore whirled around real fast and looked at me. 'That's right, Billy,' Uncle Sagamore says. 'Maybe they'll listen to you. Tell 'em just what I told – I mean, how you *seen* us take that right out of them tannery tubs. You remember.'

'Why, of course, I remember.'

'You see there?' Uncle Sagamore says to Booger. 'This here boy hisself has just told you. He *seen* us take it out of the tubs.'

Booger and Otis stared at me and then at each other, sort of disgusted. 'Ain't it awful?' Otis says. 'A young boy like that. They ort to take him away from 'em.'

'You're makin' a mistake, boys,' Uncle Sagamore says, but it didn't do any good.

They just motioned for us to get back in. Otis climbed in the back with me. When Pop stepped on the starter this time, the motor started right up, and we took off. Booger followed right close behind us in the sheriff car.

When we passed Mr Jimerson's house he was lying on the front porch in the shade with his bare feet sticking out towards the road. He raised his head up and stared at the two cars and then at Otis in the back seat of ours, and he rubbed his eyes. Then he bounced right straight up like he'd been stung by something, and started yelling, 'Prudy! Prudy! They got him! They won't run over no more of our hawgs!'

He disappeared inside the door just as we went around the bend in the road.

Pop and Uncle Sagamore was real quiet all the way to town. When we got there, Otis says, 'Go on around the square and park right in front of the courthouse.'

It was about noon by this time and the streets was pretty quiet. That is, they was at first. That sure changed in a minute. But right now there was just a few people sitting on benches under the trees, and some birds making cooing sounds high up under the roof of the courthouse. We stopped at the kerb, and Booger pulled up right behind us in the sheriff car.

There was another man with a white hat and a pistol-belt sitting on the steps leading up to the big door. Otis stuck his head out and says to him, 'Pearl, tell the sheriff to come down. We got something for him.'

Pearl jumped up and his eyes got big. He stared at Uncle Sagamore. 'You got him? You – you mean – him?' He stood there then, with his mouth open, just pointing.

Otis grinned. 'I hope to tell you we got him. We got him but good.'

Pearl whirled around and ran up the steps like a bear was after him.

Otis got out, and Booger come up from the other car. They was grinning from ear to ear. I heard somebody running along the street yelling, 'They got Sagamore Noonan. Caught him with it!'

People began to come out of the door of the courthouse and down the steps. They crowded around. More was running this way from the stores around the square. You couldn't hardly move. Pop and Uncle Sagamore and me had got out, but now we was pressed back against the car by the crowd.

'I don't believe it,' somebody says in all the jam pushing around us. 'They won't never catch Sagamore Noonan dead to rights. He's too smart for 'em.'

Somebody else says, 'The hell they won't. There he is, right there, ain't he?'

Somewhere in the back, a little kid was yelling, 'Papa, hold me up. I want to see Sagamore Noonan!

Cars going by in the street was stopping. It was jammed up from kerb to kerb. People was craning their necks. It was a regular uproar with everybody trying to talk at once, asking questions and pointing and hollering at each other.

'Is that really him?'

'Sure. The one that looks like a pirate.'

'That's Sagamore Noonan?'

'Sure, that's Sagamore Noonan.'

'I don't care what they say, they ain't got him.'

'Of course they have.'

'It'll backfire on 'em some way. You just wait.'

'I hear they found the still and ten thousand gallons of mash.'

'They caught him running off a batch.'

The little kid was screaming. 'I wanna see Sagamore Noonan. I wanna see Sagamore Noonan, I wanna see Sagamore Noonan.'

'You just wait,' a man says in the crowd right near us. 'The whole thing'll blow up right in their faces. It always does.'

I looked at him. He was a big man with a dark-complected face, wearing a baseball cap.

Another man says, 'You want to make a bet?'

'Ten dollars says he'll walk right out of there and they can't hold him. He always does,' the baseball cap man says.

'He won't this time.'

'Put your money where your mouth is,' the baseball cap man says.

'I'll take five of that,' somebody else yells.

'Here's five,' another man says, pushing through the crowd.

'Give me five too,' somebody else shouts.

Everybody was jostling and shoving and waving money. The crowd pushed us back against the car even closer. Booger nudged a man standing close to us.

'Cover all that Sagamore money you can,' he whispers. 'We got him dead to rights this time. Get down five hundred for me an' Otis if they'll bet that heavy.'

The man nodded and started pushing through the crowd. Uncle Sagamore didn't say anything. He looked real discouraged. He took off his shoes and put them in through the window of the car so he could scratch his legs with his toes, and just stood looking down at his feet. There was so much yakking you couldn't hear whether he was talking or not.

Then all of a sudden a little roly-poly man with a red face come shoving his way through the crowd like he'd been shot out of a cannon. It was the sheriff. He had his hat in his hand, wringing it the way you would a wash-cloth.

He jumped at Booger and Otis like he wanted to kiss 'em both. 'Pearl says you got him!' he yells. 'Says you caught him with the goods.'

'You bet we did,' Booger says. He pushed the people back and opened the car door. 'Look!'

The bundle of dirty clothes had been pushed off, and the top of the cardboard box was open. You could see the four fruit jars.

'Glory, glory, glory!' the sheriff yelled. 'Praise the Lord!' There was tears in his eyes and he was grinning from one ear to the other. Words just come spouting out of him.

'How did you do it, boys? How did you ever manage to catch him? We been a-tryin' for ten years! Hey, stand back, everybody! Make room for the photographer. Get the photographer down here. Get witnesses.'

Witnesses, I thought. There must have been two thousand people jammed around us in the street and on the sidewalk and the courthouse lawn.

He went right on, half-way between laughing and crying. 'Get a picture of it in the car, and then another with me holding it behind the car, so the licence plate will show. Boys, how on earth did you do it? We can confiscate the car, of course. Two whole gallons of evidence – oh boy, oh boy, oh boy. We'll put it in the safe. No, by God, I'll put it in the vault in the bank and pay the storage charges on it myself. But how in the world did you manage to outfox him?' He ran down at last.

Booger and Otis was laughing again. Booger wiped the tears out of his own eyes. 'He says it's tannery solution. Honest to God, sheriff, that's what he told us!' He broke down and howled some more. Then he got a grip on hisself and went on, 'He outsmarted hisself this time. You know what the old wart hog done?'

The sheriff began to jump up and down. 'No,' he yells. 'Of course I don't know what he done. That's what I keep asking you. What did he do?'

Booger and Otis both started talking at once. 'Well, he set fire to an old stump down there in the bottom, see? That was to draw us down there out of the way, so he could sneak out without us getting a look at his car. But we got wise as soon as we seen it was just a stump, and rushed back, and sure enough, that was what he was up to. But – but—'

They both leaned against the car, roaring fit to bust.

'But what, dammit?' the sheriff yelled.

'But the car broke down!' Booger whoops. 'So there he was, sitting there like a crippled duck, with two gallons of it on him right in broad daylight! So he tells us it's tannery solution!'

The sheriff just shook his head with the tears streaming down his cheeks. 'Boys,' he says, 'this here is the proudest day of my life. I won't never forget this.'

Uncle Sagamore mopped the sweat off his face. 'Shurf,' he says, 'I don't know what all this hooraw's about, but if your men ain't got nothin' better to do than go around pickin' on honest citizens that's trying to scratch out a livin' tanning a little leather—'

The sheriff bristled up to him like a little banty rooster. He shook a finger in his face. 'You shut up, Sagamore Noonan,' he says. 'Try to outsmart my boys, will you? Well, we got you this time.'

The photographer took pictures of the four jars and the box and then pictures of the car. A lot of people in the crowd was hollering to have the bets paid. 'There's the evidence, ain't it?' they says.

'No, sir,' others was saying. 'Bets ain't settled till we see 'em close the cell door on him. That's Sagamore Noonan, you fool. You just wait.' These ones seemed to be kind of losing heart, though. The baseball cap man was still talking loud, but it was like he wasn't quite so sure any more.

Booger picked up the box and started into the courthouse. 'Come on, Sagamore Noonan,' the sheriff says. Then he looked at Pop. 'How about this one?'

'He admitted it was his car,' Otis says.

The sheriff let out a yell. 'Glory hallelujah! Two Noonans in one haul. Come on, men.'

It looked like everybody had forgot about me. I began to be scared. They was going to draft Pop and Uncle Sagamore, and there wasn't anything I could do about it. They started pushing through the crowd, with the sheriff and the man named Pearl holding them by the arms. I followed along behind with all the people pushing around me as we went up the steps into the courthouse. We climbed some more steps to the second floor and into a big room that had 'Sheriff' wrote on a sign nailed to the door. Two girls was writing on typewriters at some desks, and there was a lot of steel cabinets with drawers in 'em. People come crowding in behind us till the whole room was full.

Booger put the box down on the desk where one of his girls was writing. Him and Pearl and Otis and the sheriff crowded around. 'Stand back a little, folks,' the sheriff was yelling. 'Give us a little room here. We got to photograph the evidence once more.'

Some of the people pushed back till they cleared a little space around his desk. Pearl motioned for Pop and Uncle Sagamore to move back towards the corner of the room. I stood close to Pop because I was still scared. There must have been twenty, thirty people in the room, all grinning, and the door was packed solid so no more could get in or out.

The photographer got his camera ready. 'Now,' the sheriff says. 'I want one shot of me opening a jar of the evidence.' He stopped then and thought about it. 'No, by golly,' he goes on, 'these two smart deputy sheriffs of mine was the ones outfoxed the old devil and caught him, so we'll all *three* have our picture made with a jar of it.'

Otis and Booger just grinned like big chessie cats. They reached in the box and each got a jar. The sheriff got one.

'Shurf,' Uncle Sagamore says, 'I keep tryin' to tell you you're makin' a mistake.'

'Shut up, Sagamore Noonan,' the sheriff says. 'We don't want to hear no more out of you.'

Uncle Sagamore scratched his leg with his big toe and looked down at the floor. 'Shucks,' he says, kind of tired and put out, 'all this hooraw over just a little old dab of tannery solution.' People just snorted at him and looked back at the sheriff.

The sheriff held up his jar and looked through. He grinned. 'Sure is a purty colour ain't she?'

Booger sat down on the corner of the desk and held his out in his hand, looking important. 'I don't never drink nothing but Old Sagamore Tannery Solution,' he says.

Everybody laughed. The photographer's flashlight went off, and all three of them started trying to twist the jars open. That glue had set, so I wondered if the caps would come off at all. They caught the bottom of the jar in one hand and the cap in the other and twisted till they made faces. Uncle Sagamore and Pop leaned back against the wall and watched, real interested.

All of a sudden the sheriff's jar just came right apart in his hands as clean as a whistle. The tannery juice went every which way, all over his clothes and the papers on the desk, and on the people standing around. It ran down his pants legs into his shoes. And before anybody could yell or jump or anything, Booger's jar did the same thing. It was just like they had been sawed in two, and it was right where Pop and Uncle Sagamore had tested them with that string. Otis's jar didn't break, but when he jumped back he dropped it and it broke all to pieces on the floor.

It was a regular madhouse. That awful smell hit everybody at the same time and they started to choke and sputter and run for the door but there was so many standing in it and in the hall outside they couldn't get through. They piled up like water piling up behind a dam. Everybody was yelling and pushing. Then the smell started to flow out through the door and people in the hall yelled and began running down the stairs. In a minute the log jam in the door broke and they all shot through at once.

Everybody, that is, but the sheriff. And of course me and Pop and Uncle Sagamore. The sheriff just stood there with his feet in a puddle of tannery juice. Papers was all over the floor, soaking up the juice, where somebody had knocked over one of the steel cabinets and spilled it open. The stuff had really spattered, like it had pressure behind it. It was on the typewriters and the desks and the walls. There was even a little dripping off the ceiling. A few drops fell on the sheriff's bald head, going spat, spat, spat. I held my nose and watched him. It was sort of odd, the way he acted.

He didn't seem to notice the smell. He just looked around real slow, and then he put his hands up over his face, and bowed his head like he was praying. In a minute he took his hands away and looked at Uncle Sagamore. His face was purple, like a cooked beet. He walked over to us, real slow, and stopped in front of Uncle Sagamore. His hands come up and made gestures like he was talking, and his mouth worked, but nothing came out.

Uncle Sagamore reached in his pocket and took out his plug of tobacco. He rubbed it on the leg of his overalls to clean it, and bit off a chew. He worked it around from one jaw into the other one, and then he says, 'Shurf, ain't you got no spittoons ir here?'

The sheriff's face was purple all the way down his neck now. His mouth went on working, but still there wasn't a sound coming out. His hands made little gestures, and with his mouth opening and closing like that it was just like watching a movie when something has happened to the sound part and the picture is still going on without it.

'Yes sir, Sam,' Uncle Sagamore says, 'it's just downright unthoughtful, that's what it is. They drag a man in here an' arrest him without no cause at all, an' they ain't even got a spittoon in the place so's he can spit. It kind of takes the heart out of a man, workin' from daylight to dark tryin' to scratch out a livin' an' pay his taxes so he can support all these goddam politicians.' He shook his head and stopped, like he'd just give up.

'It is sort of unconsiderate of 'em,' Pop says, and nods his head. He lit a cigar.

Him and Uncle Sagamore started towards the door. I followed them. The sheriff turned and watched us, and then he walked real slow back to the desk. He still hadn't been able to say a word. It was like he was all clogged up inside.

Uncle Sagamore stopped in the door and looked at him. 'Shucks,' he says, 'ain't no use holdin' hard feelin's.'

A little sound was coming out of the sheriff now. It was somelike, ' – ffffft – ssssshhhh – ffffft—'

'Hell, Shurf,' Uncle Sagamore says, 'the whole thing was just a little misunderstandin', an' I reckon I can overlook it. Matter of fact, if you want me to I won't let on to nobody it even happened. We'll just keep it a secret.'

The sheriff reached in the box and took out the last jar of the tannery juice. He held it in his hand for a minute, looking at it. Then he just drew back his arm real slow and deliberate and slammed it against the wall.

We all went out. It sure was a relief to get out in the fresh air.

We got in the car, but we didn't go home right away. Pop stopped at the grocery store and bought six pounds of baloney and some cigars. Everybody on the street was talking about the tannery juice, and they kept staring at Uncle Sagamore. He didn't seem to notice.

When we left the store we drove out in the edge of town where there was a sawmill and some railroad tracks. Uncle Sagamore showed Pop where to turn, and he drove into an alley and along it until we was in somebody's back yard.

'What are we going to do now?' I asked Pop when he stopped under a big chinaberry tree.

'Visit a friend of your Uncle Sagamore's,' he says.

Uncle Sagamore rapped four times on the door and in a minute a big woman with red hair opened it. She was wearing a kimona. She had cold blue eyes and looked like she could be plenty mean if she wanted to, but she smiled when she saw us and let us in. We followed her in through the kitchen and into another room and off to the right of it. It was kind of like a parlour, even if it was in the back of the house. Somewhere on the other side of the wall I could hear something clicking, and in a minute I figured out what it was. It was pool balls hitting each other. We was in back of a poolroom.

We sat down, she went out, and when she came back she had a big bottle and three glasses, and a bottle of coke. 'That's for you, Billy,' she says, and handed me the coke. I couldn't figure out how she knew my name.

She poured her and Pop and Uncle Sagamore a drink and then she sat down. She looked at Uncle Sagamore, and she smiled a little and shook her head. 'You'd sure never think it to look at you,' she says.

Uncle Sagamore took out his chaw of tobacco and held it in his hand while he swallowed his drink. Then he put it back in. 'Has Murph come in yet?'

'He just called,' she says. 'Said he'd be here in a minute.' Then she laughed. 'God, I'd like to seen it.'

Just then the door opened and a man come in. It was the big dark-faced man in the baseball cap that had kept saying they couldn't do anything to Uncle Sagamore. He grinned at us, and poured hisself a drink.

'Howdy, Murph,' Uncle Sagamore says. 'Did Rodey get in all right with the load?'

Murph nodded his head. 'Slick as a whistle. He was pulled off the road just the other side of Jimerson's, and as soon as he seen the two cars of you come by he went on in and loaded up. Follered you right into town. Let's see – two hundred quarts at a dollar twenty-five—'

'Two hundred and fifty dollars,' Uncle Sagamore says. 'Did you do much bettin'?'

'Six hundred and eighty, as near as I can figure it,' Murph says. 'That was includin' five hundred from Elmo Fenton, that I reckon was Booger and Otis's money.' He stopped and laughed. Then he went on, 'Let's see, that's three hundred and forty apiece. Two-fifty plus three-forty—'

'Five hundred and ninety dollars,' Uncle Sagamore says.

Murph shook his head kind of slow, like he couldn't even believe it, and began pulling money out of his pockets.

'You'd sure never think it,' he says, 'to look at you.'

Eleven

It wasn't till we'd got clear home that I remembered we hadn't took the dirty clothes to the laundry. I told Pop about it when we got out of the car.

'By golly, you're right,' he says. 'We clean forgot. Well, we'll take 'em in tomorrow or the next day. Ain't no great hurry.'

'It didn't look like it did any good at all to test those jars,' I says.

Uncle Sagamore shook his head. 'It's just gettin' to where a man can't depend on nothin' any more, I reckon. They sure don't make them jars like they used to.'

'Are you going to bottle up another batch of juice to send the gov'ment?' I asked.

Uncle Sagamore sat down on the porch and took off his shoes to think about it. 'Well sir, I don't rightly know,' he says. 'Mebbe, in a couple of days. It's just kind of disheartenin', havin' the shurf's boys break 'em up that way.'

'I think we ought to get at it right away,' I says. 'We're wasting a lot of time when we could be making some new leather.'

'This here boy's a go-getter, Sam,' he says to Pop. 'You can see he ain't goin' to let no grass grow under his feet.'

When it got along towards five o'clock they had disappeared somewhere, so I didn't have any trouble getting away to go swimming. I didn't go up by the trailer; I went straight up along the edge of the lake. Sig Freed was with me, and he kept scaring up bullfrogs. They'd go *gurk*! and make one big jump and land out in the water among the lilypads and go under. You could see Sig Freed thought they was crazy. He wouldn't even put his feet in the water hisself. Like as not, though, he just didn't know what it was. Being born and raised in a big fancy hotel there in Aqueduct, he'd probably never seen a lake like this before.

When we got up to the swimming place on the point, Miss Harrington wasn't there yet. I took off my levis and shirt and sat down on the log in my boxer shorts to wait for her. The lake was real pretty, kind of dark in the shade and smooth as glass. I looked across it and wondered if I could make it all the way without help. This was the day we was going to try it. I looked at it again, though, and decided I'd better wait for her. She'd warned me lots of times not to try swimming alone till at least the end of the summer.

It was nearly half an hour before she came along. Sig Freed barked, and then I heard her sandals in the trail. She smiled at me. She had on a blue romper suit this time, and silver sandals, and her toenails was painted red. I noticed her legs was getting tanned.

'Hello, Miss Harrington,' I says. 'Are we going to swim all the way across today?'

'Sure,' she says. 'You can make it easy.'

She took her suit out of her handbag and went off in the bushes to change. When she came back I saw it wasn't just her legs that was tanned; she was the same all over, and the diamonds on her bathing suit just glittered against this kind of golden colour she was.

'You must have been sunbathing in the raw,' I says. 'You're sure a pretty colour all over.'

She grinned at me and tousled my hair with her hand. 'Look, kid. You're seven years old, remember? Let's keep it that way.'

We waded out in the water till it was up to her waist and looked straight across. It was about fifty yards. The trees looked cool and dim along the other side because it was all in the shadow now that the sun was going down.

'You've swum this far before,' she says, 'in shallow water along the shore, and deep water's not any different at all as long as you don't get scared. So just take it slow and easy, and remember I'll be right alongside you all the way. I'm a good swimmer; I used to be in a water ballet in Florida when I was only sixteen.'

We started out, and it was as easy as pie. I dog-paddled along and she was doing a slow crawl stroke, as she called it, right beside me. When she would roll her face up out of the water on my side she'd grin at me, so I wasn't scared at all. And I could see the bushes hanging over the water on the other side getting closer all the time.

We was almost there. We didn't have more than a few feet to go and I was getting ready to reach up and grab one, when all of sudden there was an awful racket cut loose behind us on the other bank and the water began to get chopped up all around us by something. It was going *gug! gug! gug! gug!* And every time there'd be a *gug* water would fly up in a little spout like you'd throwed a rock in it. It all happened without any warning at all, and by the time I'd even figured out that the noise I was hearing over there was guns shooting real fast Miss Harrington had let out a yell and grabbed me and just pulled me under.

I'd started to yell something myself, so my mouth was open, and it got full of water. I choked, and breathed in a little before I had sense enough not to, and got water in my nose and throat. I was scared, and I started to kick and struggle trying to get back to the top, but she held me down and I could feel her kicking along like she was still swimming. We must have turned, because we went right along and didn't run into the bushes or the bank. I could still hear the things hitting up there, but down here under the water the sound was different. They went *schluck! schluck! schluck!* It was funny I even noticed it, because I was scared stiff by this time and beginning to go crazy and fight at Miss Harrington.

Just then I felt some brush, and our heads came out of the water. I took a breath, and started to choke. It seemed to me it was awful quiet, and it was a second or two before I realised what it was. The guns had stopped. I sputtered and fought for my breath, and started to look around. Overhanging limbs and leaves was all around us, there in the edge of the water. I couldn't see out across the lake at all. We stood up and started to run up onto the bank. And just then the guns cut loose again. We could hear the bullets whamming into trees a few feet off to our left. Miss

Harrington grabbed my arm and dragged me. We came shooting up onto dry ground and then stumbled and rolled across some dead leaves.

The guns cut loose again on the other side. Bullets whacked into the ground behind us and some of them glanced off trees and went screaming out ahead of us like they do in Western movies. We had our faces plastered against the ground. I was still choking and sputtering, trying to get my breath.

Then the guns stopped and I heard a couple of men yelling at each other on the other side. 'I think they got across into them trees,' one of 'em shouted. 'Come on.'

I spit out some leaves and dirt that was in my mouth, and says to Miss Harrington, 'Uncle Sagamore was right. Those rabbit hunters are sure careless where they shoot. They might of hit us.'

She clapped a hand over my mouth and pulled me up against her. She was listening for something. I couldn't hear anything except the noise we was making trying to get our breath. Then in a minute, I did. It sounded like men running through the brush on the other side of the lake.

'How far is it to the end of the lake?' She whispered in my ear.

She'd forgot she still had her hand over my mouth, I reckon. I squirmed a little, and she saw what the trouble was, and took it away. 'About a hundred yards,' I says. 'Just around the bend there.'

'We've got to get out of here,' she says, and jumps up. She grabbed me by the arm and we started running. She couldn't run very fast with no shoes on because things hurt her feet, but I was all right. I hadn't had shoes on since I'd been here. She put her feet down like she was running across egg shells, and in about a hundred yards or so we fell down again and rolled into a little gully that had ferns growing all along it.

We was both still wet and leaves and twigs was sticking to our bare skin. We was out of breath. I could hear my heart beating. She held on to me real tight, with my face against her bosom, and I could feel it going up and down when she breathed. There was ferns all around and over us.

'Don't make a sound,' she says, whispering.

'Why are we running?' I asked.

'Shhhh! Those men are looking for us. If they find me they'll kill me.'

'Kill you? You mean they ain't just rabbit hunters, like the others?'

'The others wasn't rabbit hunters, either. Hush,' she says.

It was all crazy and mixed up, I thought. Why would anybody want to hurt a nice woman like Miss Harrington? I was glad the other two had had that accident. It served 'em right. Then I began to be scared. They must be coming around the lake. Suppose they found us. I began to shake.

'Just lie still,' she whispered. 'They won't find us in these ferns.'

I laid still and listened. And in a minute I could hear them moving, running through the brush somewhere towards the head of the lake. And all of a sudden there was a shot. And then three or four in a row. And then another one by itself. There was no bullets come this way, though.

We laid real quiet in the ferns. Miss Harrington turned her face a little and looked at me. Her eyes was big and blue and worried.

'What do you reckon they're shooting at now?' I whispered.

'I'm not sure,' she says.

The sun was gone now, and it was getting shadowy out in the timber, what little of it I could see through the ferns. I wished Pop and Uncle Sagamore was there. Then we heard a sound. It was a man walking through dead leaves somewhere between us and the lake. We couldn't see him, though. We tried to hold our breath and listen, waiting to see if he was coming closer. At first it sounded that way and I was scared stiff, but before long we could tell the sound was dying out. He was going away.

'Maybe it was Pop,' I says. 'Looking for us. Or maybe Dr Severance.'

'Shhhh,' she whispered. 'I don't think so. They would have tried to call us.'

'What would they want to shoot you for?' I asked.

'Never mind,' she says. She put her hand over my mouth again.

In a few minutes we heard the steps coming back again. They went by not twenty yards away on the other side of us, it sounded like. Then they died out again.

Miss Harrington sucked in a shaky breath. 'The lousy bastards,' she says, kind of whispering.

We didn't hear anything for a long time then. It got dark. You couldn't see anything. I couldn't even see Miss Harrington's bosom, when I was lying right against it.

'I'm scared,' I says. 'I wish Pop was here.'

'I'm scared too,' she says. 'But not quite that bad.'

'They couldn't see us now,' I told her. 'Mebbe we can sort

of sneak around and get back to the house.'

'Do you know which way it is?' she asked.

'Sure,' I says. I pointed. 'That way.'

We stood up and looked around, and I wasn't so sure. It was all pitch-black, and one direction was just like another.

'Least I think it's that way,' I says. 'The lake should be right over there.'

We started out walking real slow and feeling our way, trying not to make any noise. But we kept bumping into trees and limbs. Miss Harrington hurt her feet, stepping on things.

'Damn it,' she says. 'By God, this is one for the book. This is the most. Wandering around in a crummy jungle in a G-string, with no shoes.'

'What's a G-string?' I asked.

'Nothing,' she says. 'Or next to it. *Ouch!* Goddam the crummy limbs, anyway!'

We went on. We didn't find the lake. Even if we got to it, I thought, the only way we'd know was when we walked off in it, it was so dark. Pretty soon I knew we was going the wrong way, or maybe just going around in a big circle.

And pretty soon me and Miss Harrington got separated in the dark.

'Where are you?' I called out.

'Over here,' she says.

I tried to tell by where her voice was coming from, and started that way. But then the next time she sounded further away in another direction.

'Billy,' she was saying. 'Billy, where are you?'

Then in a few minutes I couldn't hear her at all. 'Miss Harrington,' I yelled, and didn't get any answer. I was lost. And she was lost too. There was no telling which way we had been going. I got real scared and started to cry, and then I tried to run. I slammed into a tree trunk and it knocked me down. For a few minutes I just laid there and bawled like a little kid.

I didn't even have Sig Freed, and it reminded me that maybe he was lost too. There wasn't even any telling how much timber country there was down here, and maybe they never would find me or Miss Harrington.

After a while I got up and walked some more. I didn't have any idea where I was any more, or how long it had been since I'd got lost from Miss Harrington. It must have been two hours, anyway, I thought. I started to cry again, thinking about her, and just walked along with tears running down my face. Then after a while something struck me as peculiar. I wasn't running into trees any more. The stuff I was in was in rows, and it was smaller. I felt it. It was cornstalks. I must be in Uncle Sagamore's cornfield, and that was right behind the house. I stopped crying and started to run, right straight up one of the rows, feeling the long leaves brushing against me on both sides, and when I popped out of the end of it there was the house with a light burning in it.

And that wasn't all. There was a light down at the edge of the lake by Uncle Finley's ark, and a couple of cars and an ambulance and a truck, and there was six or seven men milling around. The light was coming from gasoline lanterns they was carrying. I cut down that way, still running, but I give out of breath before I got there and had to slow down to a walk.

As I came up I could see some of the men was ones I knew. There was the sheriff and Booger and Otis and Pearl. Booger and Pearl was helping another man load a stretcher into the ambulance. Uncle Sagamore and Otis and Pop was trying to unload a rowboat off the truck. It dropped, and everybody cussed. The sheriff was just standing around cussing to anybody that would listen.

I thought it was sure funny with me and Miss Harrington lost like we was that there wouldn't be at least one or two of 'em out looking for us.

I walked up to the lights. 'Hi, Pop,' I says, 'I found my way back.'

Everybody just dropped everything they was doing and swung around with their mouth open. 'Good God!' Pop says. He run over and grabbed me by the shoulders. 'Are you all right, Billy? Where the hell have you been?'

'I was lost,' I says. 'The rabbit hunters tried to shoot us, but we got out of the lake and run off down in the bottom and we got separated and it got dark and I lost Miss Harrington and after a while I found out I was walking in a cornfield, and—'

'Well!' Everybody let out a big sigh, and sat down. They all mopped their faces and shook their heads kind of slow, and looked real happy for a minute. Then doggone if everybody didn't start to cuss.

Pop and Uncle Sagamore cussed the rabbit hunters, and Pop cussed me for going swimming with Miss Harrington, and Booger and Otis and Pearl cussed Pop, and the sheriff just cussed everybody kind of impartial until he happened to remember

Uncle Sagamore and settled down to just cussing him.

'You'd know it,' he says, red-faced and rolling his hat around in his hands. 'If there was going to be a goddam war or a hurricane or a outbreak of the bubonic plague or a revolution or a rest home for city gangsters with machine-gun battles breaking out all over the place, you'd know it'd be on Sagamore Noonan's farm. It's the logical place.'

He stopped and mopped his face with the sleeve of his shirt. Then he waved an arm. 'All right, men. Load the condemned boat back on the condemned truck and if you've got all the dead gangsters in the condemned ambulance we'll get out of this condemned place. We don't have to drag the condemned lake now, because I guess there ain't anybody in it.'

He sighed and shook his head, and then went on, 'I mean there ain't anybody in it we're looking for at the moment, I'm glad we don't have to look. I'm gettin' old and I ain't got much appetite for the seamy side of life any more. There just ain't no telling, if you dragged this here peaceful lake on this peaceful little farm of Sagamore Noonan's, how many dead bodies you'd find, and old gangsters and gambling equipment, and pieces of old stills, and dope, and machine-guns, and brass knucks.'

It was like Uncle Sagamore said, I thought, the sheriff was a real excitable man. But it looked like he was forgetting that Miss Harrington was still lost.

'But, sheriff,' I says. 'We got to look for Miss Harrington. She's still down there somewhere.'

He stopped then and stared at me. He shook his head. 'That's right. I forgot about her. I don't know why – I mean, with nothing going on to interrupt a man's train of thought – but never mind. You say you got separated from her?'

'Yes, sir,' I says. 'About two hours ago, I reckon. And she can't walk very well, because she hasn't got any shoes.'

He nodded. 'I know. I know. We found all your clothes. But she's got on a bathing suit, hasn't she?'

'Yes, sir. The diamond one. But it ain't very warm, and there's not much of it to keep the mosquitoes off.'

He stared at me. 'Diamond one?'

I told him about it.

He didn't say anything for a moment. He just sighed and walked over and leaned his forehead on his arms against the side of the truck, shaking his head from side to side. In the light from the lanterns I couldn't tell if he was crying, or what. The rest of us just looked at him. Pop lit a cigar and Uncle Sagamore bit off a chaw of tobacco and looked around for a place to spit.

'If I had to grow up and be a peace officer,' the sheriff says, still with his forehead on his arms, 'why couldn't I have been born in some other county? There *is* other counties in this state. There's lots of 'em. Maybe there's even places where they ain't never heard of Sagamore Noonan. We got a big-city gang war. We got three dead gangsters. And now we got a cooch dancer lost in twenty thousand acres of river bottom with nothing on but a G-string.'

Booger and Otis and Pearl looked at each other, kind of frowning. Then the same idea seemed to hit all of 'em at once. They jumped up and started to say something, but just then the sheriff jumped too like something had bit him. He whirled around and looked at Pop and Uncle Sagamore.

'Describe this girl again,' he snaps. 'What'd you say she looked like?'

'Hmmmmm,' Pop says. 'A real doll. About five-six, I reckon. Hundred and twenty pounds, or thereabouts. Black hair, blue eyes. Mebbe twenty-one or twenty-two years old, and built sort of—'

The sheriff was real excited. 'And did she have a vine tattooed on one of her – uh—'

Pop took the cigar out of his mouth and stared at him. 'Now, how the hell would I know what she's got tattooed on her?'

'*Hah!*' the sheriff snorts. Then he whirled around to me. 'Billy, you was swimming with—'

'Why, of course she has,' I says. 'Hasn't everybody?'

The sheriff and his three men says all at the same time, '*Choo-Choo Caroline!*'

'Right here in this county all the time,' Otis says.

'And now she's lost in the river bottom,' Booger says. 'At night.'

Otis mopped his face with his handkerchief. 'In just a G-string,' he says.

Pop looked from one to the other. 'Who,' he asked, 'is Choo-Choo Caroline?'

'Nobody,' the sheriff says. 'Nobody at all. Just a striptease cooch dancer that's been on the front page of every paper in the country for the past three weeks, that's being looked for by the FBI and the police of twenty-three states, and I don't know how many different sets of gangsters. I understand they already named a new dance after her, and a television programme, and two or three different drinks, and a new type of brassiere with roses on it, and some miscellaneous underdrawers and new hair-dos and face goo and lipstick. Aside from that she's only a material witness in the biggest murder case they ever had in New Orleans, and she's been missing for three weeks with the whole United States looking for her.'

'The only thing I don't understand is why it never did occur to 'em that the only perfectly logical place for her to be is wandering around in Sagamore Noonan's river bottom in a G-string.'

Twelve

'Well sir,' Uncle Sagamore says, 'if that don't beat all.'

'We better get busy and find her,' Pop says. 'Imagine the poor girl wandering around in just that little – uh—'

Uncle Sagamore looked kind of thoughtful. 'Oh, I reckon she's safe enough down there. Ain't nothin' in that bottom that'd bother her.'

Pop started to get up. 'Well, we better organise a search party, anyway. Can't have her wanderin' around down there, scared to death, in just that little wisp of – uh—'

He caught Uncle Sagamore looking at him and didn't say no more.

The sheriff piped up then. 'Course we're goin' to start a search party,' he says. He started giving orders. He says to one of the men I didn't know, 'Harm, you take them three gangsters on into town and turn 'em over to the undertaker to hold for the inquest. Me and Pearl and Otis and Booger will stay here. We got three lanterns between us. Doughbelly, you drive the truck back with the rowboat. Get hold of Robert Stark. Tell him to round up twenty men – not no more because if we get this bottom full of people we'll spend as much time looking for lost searchers as we will for her. Tell him to requisition Rutherford's sound truck, the one they use during campaigns. If we make enough noise up here, she may find her way in by herself. Tell everybody to bring gasoline lanterns or flashlights. All right, get movin'.'

The fat one nodded his head and started to get in the truck. 'May have a little trouble gettin' twenty men, this time of night.'

'Just tell 'em what she's wearin',' the sheriff says. 'You won't have no trouble at all.'

Pop and Uncle Sagamore just looked at each other again.

The sheriff waved his hand. 'Oh, yes. Tell Robert Stark to call the state prison farm for the dawgs. They can have 'em here by noon tomorrow, if we ain't found her by that time.'

The truck and the ambulance drove away. Pop motioned for me to come along, and him and Uncle Sagamore went up to the house. We all sat down on the front porch.

'Where's Dr Severance?' I asked. 'And what did the sheriff mean about three dead gangsters? And where's Sig Freed? And why was they going to drag the lake?'

Uncle Sagamore didn't say a word. He just sat there wiggling his toes like he was thinking. Pop told me all about it.

They heard the shooting, and went over there and found our clothes where we'd left them on the log, so they figured the men had shot us and we was lying on the bottom of the lake. They called the sheriff from Mr Jimerson's house. And when the sheriff's men got there they found Dr Severance up near the head of the lake. He was dead. And right near him there was two other dead men with tommy guns. They was the ones that tried to shoot us. I felt bad about Dr Severance, but I figured the other ones got just what was coming to them.

'Hey, Pop,' I said then, 'there must have been three of them.' I told him about the one we heard while we was hiding in the ferns.

'Hmmmmm,' Pop says. 'Well, likely he's already give up and left, unless he's lost, too. Anyway, I reckon he didn't find her, because there ain't been no more shootin'.'

'Well, you reckon the sheriff's men will find her all right?' I asked. I was worried about her.

'Sure,' Pop says.

Uncle Sagamore still looked like he was thinking. There was a little light coming out the window from the lamp inside, and I could see him working his tobacco around in his mouth, from one cheek to the other. He spit. 'Reckon they will, at that. Likely a good chance of it,' he says.

'I expect you're right,' Pop says. He looked thoughtful too.

I could see the three lanterns the sheriff and his men was carrying start down towards the timber on the lower side of the lake. Pop and Uncle Sagamore stayed kind of quiet for a minute.

'By God,' Pop says then.

'Ain't she a beauty?' Uncle Sagamore asked.

'She sure is,' I said. I thought they meant Miss Harrington. I told them how she looked all tanned like that with her diamond bathing suit glittering. They looked at each other.

Pop choked on his cigar smoke. 'Hush,' he says.

'Yes sir, by God,' Uncle Sagamore says. 'It's what you would call a natural situation. You couldn't even start out and build one like it.'

'Stacked, famous, nakid, and lost,' Pop says.

'She ain't nekkid,' I says. 'She's got on her bathing suit.'

'Damn it, Billy,' Pop snaps at me. 'Will you hush up for a minute? A man don't live through many moments like this in his life, and he don't want 'em spoiled with noise.'

'Yes sir, just think of it,' Uncle Sagamore says.

'Kind of makes little cold chills run up your back, don't it?' Pop asked. Then he went on, kind of discouraged. 'But like you say, they'll likely find her before morning.'

'Gosh, I sure hope so,' I says. They didn't let on like they even heard me.

'A man couldn't hardly get started with nothin' by that time,' Pop says.

'That's right,' Uncle Sagamore said to him. 'He'd have to give guarantees, to do any dickerin' with anybody.'

I didn't know what they was talking about. And then I suddenly remember I still hadn't found out anything about Sig Freed.

'Where's Sig Freed?' I asked Pop.

'I don't know,' he says. 'I thought he was around here.'

'Have you seen him lately?'

Pop thought about it. 'No. I reckon we ain't, now that you mention it. Mebbe he went off looking for you.'

'You don't suppose those people would hurt him, do you?' I asked. 'He was there where we was swimming.'

'No, ain't no reason they'd do a thing like that,' Pop says. 'Now stop worryin'. A dawg can find his way back all right.'

I got up. 'Well, I'm going to take a look around.'

'Don't you go far,' Pop says. 'I don't want you to git lost again.'

'I won't,' I says.

I walked up towards the big house trailer, calling 'Sig Freed! Here, Sig Freed!' It was awful dark and I couldn't see much, but I knew if he heard me he'd bark and come running. I didn't get any answer from him, though. I came back down past Uncle Finley's ark, and then cut back up the hill towards the front yard, meaning to go down past the barn and yell in that direction. Pop and Uncle Sagamore was still sitting on the front porch, talking.

'I can't find him,' I says.

'Hell, don't worry,' Pop says. 'You can't lose a dawg.'

I wasn't so sure, though. 'But, Pop, he's a city dog.'

I started to go on across the yard, and then doggone if I didn't hear him. It sounded like he was down the other side of the barn in the edge of the trees. He was barking.

'That's him, Pop,' I says, and started to run down that way.

And then Uncle Sagamore and Pop both bounced off the porch. Pop caught my arm. 'Wait a minute, Billy,' he says. 'Hold it.'

'Why?' I asked. 'That's Sig Freed, all right. I know his bark.'

'Sure,' Uncle Sagamore says. 'That's him, sure enough. But you ain't been around dawgs as long as I have. That there's a skunk bark, sure as you're born.'

'Just what I was thinkin',' Pop says. He still was holding me by the arm. 'When I heard it, I says to myself, that there dawg's treed a skunk.'

'Well, maybe so,' I told him. 'But we can't just leave him down there to let the skunk stink him up.'

'You better let Sagamore take care of it,' Pop says. 'He knows how. You just sit right here and wait.'

'But, Pop—'

'Never you mind. You just do like I tell you. I don't want you all stunk up with polecat. You'd have to go off and live in the barn.'

Uncle Sagamore started walking down towards the barn real fast. Pop and me sat down on the porch. We could hear Sig Freed still barking, and it didn't sound like he was too far the other side of the barn.

Nothing happened for a few minutes. Then Sig Freed's bark changed a little, and in a minute he let out a yip and stopped barking altogether.

Uncle Sagamore yelled something.

Pop walked out by the well and called back, 'What? What you say?'

'Call the dawg,' Uncle Sagamore yelled. 'Git him up there and keep him.'

'Here, Sig Freed!' I called. 'Sig Freed! Sig Freed!'

In a minute he came running up. He jumped up in my arms and started licking my face. 'He didn't get no skunk on him, Pop,' I says. 'See, he smells just like he always did.'

'Well, that just goes to show you,' Pop says. 'Sagamore knows how to handle one. Better hold on to that dawg, though. Don't let him go back down there.'

We sat down on the porch again and I held Sig Freed by his collar. He was real happy. It seemed like a long time went by, though, and Uncle Sagamore didn't come back.

'You reckon he's having trouble with the skunk?' I asked.

'Sagamore having trouble with one crummy little old skunk?' Pop says. 'Not on your life. He's a match for any skunk that ever come down the pike. He'll be back in a minute.'

Some more time went by, and I started worrying again about Miss Harrington. She'd be awful scared down there by herself. 'Hadn't we all ought to go down there and help look for her?' I asked Pop.

He shook his head. 'Ain't much we could do,' he says. 'And I don't want you gettin' lost again.'

Just then Uncle Sagamore came around the corner of the house. He sat down on the step in the dark and bit off a chaw of tobacco. 'Well sir, by golly,' he says. 'It was just like we thought.'

'Well, you can generally tell, by the bark, if you know dawgs,' Pop says. 'You didn't have no trouble?'

'Hmmmm,' Uncle Sagamore says. 'Not overly much. Skunks is a lot like mules and wimmin. You just got to reason with 'em. You ain't goin' to git nowhere givin' orders to a skunk, but if'n you take the time to explain the whole thing to him he'll generally see it yore way.'

'You reckon it's safe to turn the dawg loose now?' Pop asked.

'Oh, sure. He ain't going to locate him now. Let him go.'

I turned Sig Freed loose. He ran around out in the dark in the front yard, but he didn't go far.

Uncle Sagamore sailed out some tobacco juice. You couldn't see it, but you could hear the *ka-splott* when it landed. 'You know, Sam,' he says. 'I'm sorta worried about that there girl.'

'Well,' Pop says, 'I have been, too, but I just didn't want to let on.'

'Oh,' Uncle Sagamore says, 'she ain't in no danger. They ain't nothin' down there that'd hurt her, mind you. But it's just that she'll get scared, all alone like that, and the muskeeters is goin' to chaw on her somethin' awful, being light dressed like she is.

Sam, you reckon the shurf's handlin' this thing just the way he ort? With only twenty men?'

'Just what I was thinkin', myself,' Pop says. 'It seems to me like the shurf just ain't got a real grasp of the situation. Now, if it was me—'

'If it was me,' Uncle Sagamore says, 'I'd offer a reward.'

'Why, of course,' Pop went on. 'And kinda let people know about it.'

'Natcherly. I'd distribute a few hand bills and mebbe call the papers. Sort of describe her, how she looks and how she was dressed the last time anybody saw her, so people'd know what to look for. I reckon we could get out a pretty good description of the girl, now couldn't we?'

'Ho-ly hell. I mean, of course we could. We seen her around often enough, ain't we?'

'Well sir, I'll tell you,' Uncle Sagamore says. 'I just ain't satisfied with the way the shurf's handlin' this thing. That there girl's a good friend of ours, an' Billy sets all the store in the world by her, an' here that shurf's going to go a-piddlin' around down there with a little old dab of men that couldn't find a dead mouse in a glass of buttermilk, while she works herself up into a swivet and gets bit all to hell by the muskeeters. It just don't seem right to me.'

'Well, then, what do you reckon we ort to do?' Pop asked.

'Now, mind you,' Uncle Sagamore says, 'I'd be the last one in the world to want to interfere with the workin's of the law, but it shore seems to me like it's our duty to let the people know what's goin' on down here so we can get more help to look for her. People'd come a-runnin' if they knew the facts, 'specially when they heard about the reward.'

'Hmmmm!' Pop says. 'Mebbe about two hundred?'

'Better make it five hundred,' Uncle Sagamore decided.

'Say, that's fine,' I told them. 'We'll get lots of help. Who'll pay it?'

'Shucks, ain't no use worryin' about that now,' Uncle Sagamore says. 'The thing to do now is find that there girl. Plenty of time later on to worry about piddlin' little details.'

'Well, what are we waitin' for?' Pop says. He jumped up. 'We got a printing press out there in the trailer, haven't we? And hundreds of pounds of paper. Come on, Billy. Let's get to work.'

'Sure,' I says.

We got a lantern and went out to the trailer. Pop closed the door and sat down at the little desk with a sheet of paper and a pencil. 'You start settin' her up as fast as I get it wrote out,' he says. 'We don't want to lose no time.'

He opened the little dictionary and started looking up the words. Pop can't spell anything without looking it up.

It was hot inside the trailer, but we was too busy to notice.

Pop got the lead-off blocked out the way he wanted it and I set it up in big type, and then he started with the rest of it, the description and how to find the place and everything

While we was working there was a sound like a horse outside and we looked out

Uncle Sagamore had saddled one of his mules, and he was setting on his back with something that looked like a bundle of clothes under his arm

'How you makin' out, Sam?' he asked.

'Fine,' Pop says. 'We'll be ready to start printing her in a few minutes. You goin' down in the bottom?'

'That's right,' Uncle Sagamore says. 'I figured I ort to help the boys out, seein' as how I can't do nothin' here.'

'What's that you got in your arms?' I asked Uncle Sagamore.

'Oh,' he says. 'I went up to the trailer an' found a suit of Miss Harrington's clothes. We find her, she'll want something to wear.'

I hadn't thought of that. It was a good idea.

We closed the door and started to work again.

Pop was chewing on his pencil. 'Hmmmmm! Twenty-two years old—' he says, talking to hisself. 'No. Better make that nineteen. Get a sportier type of searcher. Now. Which bosom is that vine on?'

'The off one,' I says, reaching for more type. 'And right in the centre it's got a little, pink—'

'Damn it, Billy—' He wiped the sweat off his face. 'Never mind.' He sighed and went on muttering. 'Climbing rose – golden suntan all over – hips – God, if I don't stop readin' this thing over while I'm writin' it, I'll be down there lookin' for her myself.'

In a little while he had it all wrote out the way he wanted it, and I finished setting it up in type. I inked it and ran off one to see how it was.

Pop looked at it. 'Well, that sure enough ought to fetch 'em,' he says. 'I'll have to save one to show to Sagamore. It's a down-right work of art.'

I read it over, and it sure sounded fine, all right.

REWARD!!

NUDE GIRL LOST IN SWAMP!!

REWARD! $500 REWARD!

MISS CHOO-CHOO CAROLINE,
FAMOUS BUBBLE DANCER, LOST

Five hundred dollars in cash will be paid for the safe return of Miss Choo-Choo Caroline, world-famous strip-tease dancer, lost in wild river bottom back of the Noonan farm five miles south of the town of Jerome, in Blossom County.

Miss Caroline has been missing since 5 P.M. Tuesday evening, when she was surprised, attacked, and shot at by gangsters while in swimming clad in only a diamond G-string. She is known to have escaped into the timber at that time, but will shortly be suffering from exposure due to having no clothes on.

Description:

Bust	36
Waist	24
Hips	36

Winner of three beauty contests, water ballet star at 16, former model, Queen of the Water Ski Festival in 1955. Lovely, breath-taking brunette with deep blue eyes and jet black hair. Nineteen years old. Smooth golden suntan all over. May be identified by tattoo in the form of a rambler rose entwined around right breast with small pink flower in centre.

PLEASE HELP US FIND THIS GIRL!

Thirteen

We started rolling it out. I cranked till my arm was wore out, and then Pop took over. We stacked the sheets in big blocks and then put them in a cardboard box. When the box was full we started another one. Pop got tired and I took over again. Pop got a road map out of the car and sat down at the little desk, marking off the towns all around and the best way to make 'em all with one sweep. He kept looking at his watch.

We was filling up the second box when we began hearing cars outside.

'All right, I think we got enough,' Pop says. 'Put out the lantern.'

I blew it out, and we went outside. Pop closed the door. There was three cars parked just up the hill from the front yard, and another one was coming. In its headlights I could see one of the others was a sound truck, with a big loudspeaker mounted on top. Men began to get out and light lanterns.

'Which way?' a man yells at Pop.

Pop was standing in a headlight beam. He swung his arm and pointed towards the bottom. 'Down there,' he says.

Men started hurrying down the hill, running around the corners of the house and out towards the cornfield with their lanterns. 'Hey, you guys, wait for me,' others was calling out from the cars.

Pop lit a cigar. 'Sure is a enthusiastic search party,' he says. 'But they're goin' to need help. I can just feel it.'

The loudspeaker on the truck began to make noise. It let out a big blast and says, '*Wheeeet! Wheeeet!* Testing, one, two, three, four. Testing. Up this way, Miss Caroline. Follow the music.'

It started playing a record. It was sure loud. I reckon you could of heard it over a mile.

'Hey, Pop,' I says. 'That'll bring her in in no time, if she can still walk. That's a good idea.'

'Sure is.' Pop nodded his head. 'But it's a awful big bottom down there. Three or four miles across. Even so, they ort to find her by daylight.'

'Reckon we ought to go ahead and distribute them hand bills?' I asked.

'Oh, sure,' he says. 'Got to do everything we can to help out.

By the way, though, if I was you I wouldn't mention nothing about them to the shurf. Them beaurocrats always want to run things their own way, an' they get all fussed when somebody like a ordinary citizen tries to help out.'

'Sure,' I says. 'I won't say nothing.'

All the men was gone from the cars now except the one playing the records in the sound truck. Pop reached in the trailer and took out the two boxes of hand bills and carried them up to our car.

Just as we was putting them in the seat Uncle Sagamore rode up on his mule. I could just barely see him in the dark. He had to get down to talk, because the record playing in the sound truck made so much noise.

'You about ready to go, Sam?' he asked.

'Just startin' now,' Pop says. 'How is the search goin'?'

'I made one sweep down across the bottom an' back, but didn't see a sign of her. Didn't even see any of the searchers. Lots of ground down there.'

Pop got in the car and leaned his head out the window. 'They're goin' to need all the help they can get, an' that's a fact,' he says. 'By the way, here's one of the hand bills.'

Uncle Sagamore struck a match and read it. 'Hmmm,' he says. 'Sure got a nice ring to it. Matter of fact, I reckon you better get everybody lined up an' tell 'em to be in here by daylight, before you throw many of them things around. Might not even get in, if they don't hurry.'

'Can I go with you, Pop?' I asked.

They both turned around like they'd forgot I was there. 'Say,' Pop says, 'you go on up there and unroll your bed and get some sleep.'

'But Pop—'

'You do like I tell you. And don't you go off down in that bottom any more. I'll bring you some jaw-breakers.'

'All right,' I says. I went back and sat down on the step with Sig Freed. Pop and Uncle Sagamore talked for about five minutes more, and then Pop drove off. Uncle Sagamore came back down through the yard, leading the mule. He sat down on the step next to me to rest for a minute.

'You might as well go to bed,' he says. 'Ain't no use you stayin' up.'

Just then Uncle Finley came tearing out through the door in his nightshirt. He was barefooted, and his bald head was shining in the lamplight coming through the window.

'What's that there awful racket?' he yells. 'How's a man goin' to get any sleep, with all that bellerin' an' screechin'?'

Uncle Sagamore spit real careful and wiped his mouth with the back of his hand. 'Why, that there's just the shurf's sound truck, Finley,' he says. 'Ain't nothin' to get excited about. Seems like there's a nakid cooch dancer wanderin' around out there an' he's tryin' to toll her in.'

'I knowed it,' Uncle Finley says. 'Just what you'd expect around this here place. Nothin' but sin. Everybody's goin' to drowned. Cooch dancers runnin' in an' out of the bushes a-shakin' theirselves at people, an' horns a-honkin' all hours of the day an' night so decent people can't sleep. It's a comin'. The day's a comin', an' it ain't going' to be long. You're gonna see 'em come pourin' in here beggin' to be let aboard, but I ain't going to take 'em. Not a one.'

'Well sir,' Uncle Sagamore says, 'that sure is rough on the rest of us, but if that's the way you and the vision got her figured, I reckon that's the way it's got to be. If it was me, though, doggone if I wouldn't try to squeeze over and make room for that there cooch dancer, anyway. She wouldn't take up much space, an' she could sit in your lap.'

Uncle Finley says, 'Hmmmmmph!' and went back in the house.

Uncle Sagamore got on his mule and went back around the house towards the bottom. The sound truck went on playing music, and every once in a while the man would talk into the microphone. 'This way, Miss Caroline. Follow the sound.'

Then there would be another record.

I stretched out on my bedroll and tried to get some sleep, but the loudspeaker made so much noise I didn't have any luck. I got to worrying about Miss Harrington, down there all alone and scared, with her feet sore and the mosquitoes biting her, and that didn't help any either. But I'd promised Pop I wouldn't go back and look for her any more tonight, so I didn't. I would of gone anyway in spite of the promise, if I'd thought it would do any good, but I didn't see how I could find her if over twenty men couldn't.

It was funny, I thought, that I kept calling her Miss Harrington even after the sheriff and his men said her name was Choo-Choo Caroline. I wondered what a cooch dancer was, and what a material witness was, but I figured there wasn't either one of 'em very bad, even if the police had been looking for her. It must have been that Dr. Severance had been hiding her from those gangsters so they couldn't shoot her. I felt sorry about him.

I must have dozed off after a while, but when I woke up it was still dark. Sig Freed was lying beside me on the bedroll, and he was growling. Somebody was coming around the corner of the house. I looked at Pop's bedroll to see if he had come back yet, but it was empty. The man walked on through the front yard and sat down on the top step close to my feet. The lamp was still burning in the front room, and I could see it was the sheriff out there.

'Billy, you asleep?' he asked.

'No,' I says. 'Have you found her yet?'

He took off his hat and mopped his head, and slumped down a little like he was real tired. 'Not a sign of her. God, I'm wore out. Feel like I'd walked a hundred miles through that brush.'

'Is everybody still looking?' I asked.

'Everybody except me an' Otis. We're goin' back to town to get a few hours' sleep an' bring out a fresh party to relieve these around ten this morning. It's three-thirty now, an' it looks like we ain't goin' to find her as soon as I thought.'

'Sure funny you ain't,' I says. 'But then, Uncle Sagamore says that's a awful big bottom down there.'

'It sure as hell *is* funny,' he says. 'Don't make no difference how big the place is. She couldn't of gone very far barefooted. When her feet got sore she'd sit and stay where she was.'

'It seems like it to me, too,' I says.

'Billy,' he says. 'I want to ask you something, and I want you to tell me the truth. Was that girl really with you when you ran off down there? When they shot at you, I mean?'

'Of course she was,' I said. I sat up in bed.

'Are you sure she didn't get – uh – shot, there in the water? And you got scared and didn't want to tell anybody?'

'No. What would I want to tell a story about it for? Heck, she was the one pulled me out of the water.'

I told him the whole thing, how Miss Harrington had towed me along until we got under the bushes, and how we'd run off down the hill and hid in the ferns.

He shook his head. 'Well, I reckon it must be true. But I'll be damned if I can see how she got so far away twenty men can't find her.'

'I don't understand it, either,' I says.

'Well, when I get back in the morning, will you go with me and see if you can point out this place where you hid in the ferns?'

'Sure,' I says. 'We can go now, if you want to.'

'No, we'll wait for daylight,' he says. He sighed and kind of stretched out a little. 'I couldn't walk that far, nohow. I'm pooped. Say, where's Sagamore?'

'He's down in the bottom, looking for her. He went off that way on his mule.'

'Hmmmph,' the sheriff says. 'That don't sound like him a bit. You mean he's actually goin' to do something useful, after fifty years?'

Just then Otis come around the corner of the house, and him and the sheriff went on up and got in their car. They drove off. The sound truck started another record.

In about half an hour I heard Uncle Sagamore's truck start up, down there by the barn. It went up the hill towards the wire gate. I wondered where he was going this time of night. After a while I heard the motor racing like he was stuck in the sand. That went on for five or ten minutes, and then it stopped. Pretty soon he came back, walking.

He came up on the steps. 'What happened to the truck?' I asked.

'Oh, he says. 'I got stuck in the sand. Daggone truck just bogged down like a heifer in a mudhole.'

'That's too bad,' I says. 'You didn't see any sign of Miss Harrington down in the bottom?'

'Not a trace. But I reckon they'll find her, come daylight.'

He went on down towards the barn, and after a while I went to sleep. I didn't wake up again till it was broad daylight, and it was beginning. I never saw anything like it my life.

Even before I opened my eyes I knew they had brought the tubs back. The smell was in my nose before I was full awake, and Sig Freed was sniffing and whimpering about it beside me on the bedroll. When he saw me open my eyes he licked me on the face. The sound truck had stopped making noise, but I could see it still sitting up there, about fifty yards from the house. I rolled over the other way, to see if Pop was there. His bedroll had been slept in, but he was gone. I didn't hear any sounds in the house, though, like they was cooking breakfast.

Our car was parked under the tree in front, and beyond it was the four cars the searchers had come in. But there wasn't anybody around. I walked up to the sound truck, and the man in it was asleep. I wondered where Pop and Uncle Sagamore had gone. Then I decided maybe they'd gone down in the bottom to help look for Miss Harrington. Not Harrington, I thought. Caroline. I ought to get used to calling her by her right name. Then I wondered if I'd ever see her again. Maybe they never would find her. That scared me, and I thought, sure, what the heck, of course they'll find her.

I just remembered we hadn't had any supper last night, so after I went down to the lake to wash up, I started a fire in the stove to fry some baloney. While I was putting the lids back on it, Uncle Finley came out of his room, putting on his tie and tucking the end of it inside the bib of his overalls.

'Where's everybody at?' he asked, giving me a hard stare like maybe I'd ate 'em or something.

'I don't know,' I says. I went on slicing baloney and putting it in the pan.

'Off a-lookin' for that there cooch dancer,' he says. 'Everybody up to devilment, all the time.' He stopped and looked at me. 'I heard tell she ain't got no clothes on.'

'Well, she ain't got much,' I says. 'The mosquitoes is probably chewed her something fierce.'

'Hmmmmph,' he says. 'The way I heered it, she ain't got on a stitch. Shameless hussy. You ain't seen her around, have you?'

'No sir,' I says. Uncle Finley always scared me a little. He looked like a man shouting at something nobody else could see.

'Well, she's a-goin' to drowned, as sure as hell,' he says.

'She won't neither drowned,' I says. 'She's a good swimmer.'

'Hmmmmph,' he says. He sat down at the end of the table with his knife sticking up in one hand and the fork in the other, waiting for the baloney. When it was fried, I put it on the table and we both ate.

There was a sound then like a truck or something up on the hill by the wire gate. We went out through the front room to look up that way. Uncle Finley was in the lead, and when he got to the door leading out onto the porch, he stopped for a second and stared like he'd seen a miracle.

'Lumber!' he shouted.

He made one big leap and landed clear out in the yard, and started running, still shouting, 'Lumber!' at every other jump. I looked up that way to see what it was had excited him that way. I couldn't hardly believe my eyes.

There was a truck, all right, coming down from the direction of the gate, and I could see it was stacked with lumber, but it was the trucks behind it I was staring at. There was three of them right behind the one with the lumber, and while I was looking another one came into sight. They was yellow trucks, and they had big signs painted on them. They was piled high with what looked like canvas tents folded up.

'Come on,' I yelled to Sig Freed, and we started up there on the run.

We scooted past the sound truck, and then I saw Pop was up there. He was walking along beside the front one of the yellow trucks, and he motioned for them to pull off in an open place beside the ruts about a hundred yards away. He waved for the one with the lumber to pull off on the other side.

The one with the lumber stopped, but Uncle Finley was already there, and before the men could even get out he ran around back and pulled off a board about twenty feet long and started running down the hill towards the ark, dragging the board after him.

'Hey,' the men in the truck yelled, and took out after him. One of them got hold of the end of the board and started trying to take it away from him.

The other one yelled at Pop, 'Who's this crazy old bastard? Tell him to leave this lumber alone.'

Pop was telling the drivers of the yellow trucks where to park. He looked around and waved a hand. 'That's just Finley. Let him have the plank and he won't bother you no more. He'll be all day nailing it up.'

The two men let go the plank and Uncle Finley went scooting down towards the ark, letting the end of it drag behind him. They came back to the truck and began unloading the rest of it on the ground.

I was close enough to the yellow trucks now to read the signs. They said 'Burke's Shows'. It was a carnival! Going to be set up right on Uncle Sagamore's farm.

Fourteen

I looked behind them. There was more coming. And some big yellow trailers with 'Burke's Shows' on the side of them. And then some cars. And then a big shiny aluminium house trailer. And then more cars. They was just pouring down the hill from the gate with dust boiling up everywhere. They ran right on past the house and across the cornfield, and when they hit the edge of the timber they stopped and men began to jump out. They took off into the trees.

They'd sure find Miss Harrington now, I thought. It looked like the whole world had turned out to look for her.

I ducked across when there was an open space between cars so I could get through, and ran up to where Pop was. He was still waving his arms and motioning to the drivers of the trucks. They was backing them here and there, and as soon as one was in the right spot men jumped down and began unloading the big tents. Other men had axes and was cutting down the little trees and bushes in the way.

'Hey, Pop,' I yelled as I came up, 'where did the carnival come from?'

He looked around at me, and went on motioning to one of the drivers. 'Careful of them cars, Billy,' he says. 'Don't get run over.'

'But, Pop,' I says, getting out of the way so a truck could swing up past me, 'how'd they happen to bring a carnival way out here?'

'Don't bother me now,' he says. 'I'll talk to you after a while. And you watch out for them cars.'

I was jumping up and down, I was so excited about the carnival. Sig Freed was excited too, and he began running around in big circles, getting in the way.

'Get that dawg out of here before he gets run over,' Pop yelled. 'Go on down to the lake or somewhere. You can come back after it's all set up.'

I could see the gate from here, and when I looked up the hill I saw Uncle Sagamore. He was standing there beside it, with all the cars going past him. I could see some sort of sign nailed up on one of the posts, but this far away I couldn't tell what it said. I called Sig Freed and we ran up that way to see what he was doing.

When I got a little closer, I could make out the sign. It said

'Noonan Farm. Parking $1.00.' Uncle Sagamore was standing across from it, on the drivers' side of the cars, with a flour sack. Every time a driver would turn out of the road and in through the gate he would hand Uncle Sagamore a dollar. Uncle Sagamore would drop it in the flour sack and wave for him to go on.

It seemed to me like a dollar was pretty high to pay for parking way out here in the country where there was thousands of acres, and I wondered why a lot of them didn't just drive on down the road and pull off somewhere further along. Heck, they only charged fifty cents at most race tracks.

Then, when I got up to the gate I saw why they was all turning in. The road going on past was blocked. Uncle Sagamore's truck was broke down right square in the middle of it less than a car's length past where our ruts turned off through the gate. It looked like he had tried to turn it around and had got lodged between the trees growing up on both sides. It was jammed in for fair, with the front axle against a stump on one end and the tail-gate between two trees on the other. And on top of that, one of the back wheels was missing, like he'd had a flat tyre and started to change it. There just wasn't any way you could move that truck without cutting down the trees on both sides or taking it apart and carrying it away in a wheelbarrow.

And they couldn't get out of the road anywhere back the other way for at least a hundred yards. There was solid pine trees on both sides, plus Uncle Sagamore's wire fence along this edge of it. I looked up that way, and it was just jammed with cars, bumper to bumper. They was going slow because each car had to give Uncle Sagamore a dollar, and that jammed them up behind. Some of them was honking their horns, and men was yelling, wanting to know what the trouble was.

Just as I walked up alongside Uncle Sagamore the car making the turn stopped, but the driver didn't hold out a dollar. He was a big red-faced man with a white moustache and there was another man in the front seat with him.

The man driving jerked his head at the sign and then shouted at Uncle Sagamore. 'You think I'm going to pay a dollar to park out here in the country? You're nuts.'

The other man in the seat jabbed him with his elbow, and whispers, 'Shhhh! Hush, you dam' fool. That's Sagamore Noonan.' He was a real skinny man with a big Adam's apple that kept on going up and down when he talked.

'I don't give a goddam who he is,' the red-faced one says. 'I ain't going to pay no dollar to park.'

Cars behind was beginning to blow their horns at the delay. Somebody stuck his head out back down the line. 'Hey, what the hell's the matter with you guys up there? You want 'em to find her before we get there?'

'Shut up!' The red-faced one shouted. 'This here bandit's tryin' to hold us up.'

Uncle Sagamore spit and wiped his mouth with the back of his hand, real thoughtful. Then he reached down by the gate post for something. By golly, it was his shotgun. I hadn't seen it before. He hefted it once and slid the safety catch back and forth, and then leaned on the car window with it across his arm. The end of the barrel was sticking right in the big man's face. Only his face wasn't red now. It was white, and getting whiter by the second. Big drops of sweat collected on his forehead.

Uncle Sagamore cocked his ear around a little by turning his head like a deaf person, and says, 'How was that again? Them horns back there was makin' so much noise I didn't quite catch what you was sayin'.'

'Oh,' the big man says. 'Oh, I was – uh – just sayin' I sure hope we find that there girl.' He took a dollar bill out of his pocket and reached it out real careful like it might blow up in his face.

Uncle Sagamore took it and waved for him to go on. Cars kept right on coming. I never saw money pouring into anything like the dollars pouring into his flour sack. It was just like a two-dollar window on Saturday. Sometimes a man would give him a five or a ten, and Uncle Sagamore would just reach down inside the sack and come out with a wad of ones as big as a hat to count out the change. Then he'd stuff the rest back in, along with the five or the ten. Silver coins went right in the sack along with the paper money.

One or two more started to give him an argument, so he just kept the shotgun in the crook of his arm. It saved picking it up each time, and it seemed like it also cut down on the arguments a lot too. There was no way the cars could back up, if they didn't want to pay, because they was bumper to bumper way back as far as you could see, and there wasn't room to turn around. So they just had to come on in, and when they did they had to pay. I could see Uncle Sagamore was going to make a fortune if this lasted very long. The sack was already beginning to bulge and rattle at the bottom.

In nearly all the cars somebody would stick his head out as they came through, and ask, 'They found her yet?'

For a while Uncle Sagamore would say, 'No. Not yet.' Then he took to just saying, 'No.' And finally he quit even that and just shook his head.

A truck come through carrying ice and tubs and cases of pop and a big icebox and a stove. The man driving it was Murph. Uncle Sagamore waved him on through without the dollar, and says, 'They're buildin' the stand down there now across from the carnival.'

Murph nodded. 'Looks like a good crowd.'

Murph drove on in. I could see there wasn't any chance of talking to Uncle Sagamore as long as he was busy raking in money like that, so I ran down the hill alongside the truck. It pulled up on the left-hand side of the road where they had unloaded the lumber. This was near Dr Severance's trailer, and there wasn't many trees from here on down to the house, about a hundred yards. Right across the road they was putting up the carnival tents. They had one of the big ones partly up now, and there was a raised ticket stand and a little stage out in front that had a big sign over it that said 'Girls! Girls! Girls!' It didn't look like they had a Ferris wheel or even a merry-go-round, though.

Murph stopped the truck and got out. The whole place was in an uproar now and it sounded and looked like a big day at a race track. You'd think it was the Preakness, or something. Cars was whizzing on down the hill and past the house, out into the cornfield. Men was shouting and struggling with the tents over there, and now a bunch of girls was beginning to come out of one of the trailers, all dressed in romper suits. The two men that had unloaded the lumber was trying to nail together what looked like a hot-dog stand out of it.

They had the outline of it started, up about two planks high nailed to 2-by-4's at the corners, but every time they'd pick up a board and start to nail it up, turning their back on the lumber pile, Uncle Finley would swoop down and grab a plank and light out for the ark They'd have to drop theirs and chase him and rassle it away from him

Murph lit a cigarette and looked around. 'Good God,' he says. 'What a boar's nest. Be ten thousand people here by noon, the way they're pouring in.'

'They sure ought to find her,' I says.

'What?' he asked. 'Oh. Sure. Hell, there won't even be room for her down in that bottom in another two hours, unless she sits on somebody's shoulder.'

The two men come up with the plank and put it back on the pile. Uncle Finley stood off a little ways and watched them.

'Shake it up, you guys,' Murph says. 'We got to get in operation here so we can feed all them hungry heroes when they come up out of the bottom.'

'Well, how the hell can we get anything done,' one of them says, 'with that old crackpot stealing the planks faster than we can nail 'em up? What the hell's the matter with him, anyway?'

'I don't know,' Murph says. 'Mebbe he thinks he's a termite.' He started lifting the tubs down and breaking up ice in them for the bottles of pop.

Then he looked across the road to where the girls that had come out of the trailer was standing around lighting cigarettes and waving at the men going by in cars. 'Hmmmm,' he says. 'Not a bad-looking bunch of pigs he rounded up. They ought to pull 'em in. You know, kid, I've seen some operators in my day, but he's the most.'

'Who's that?' I asked.

'Who else? Your Uncle Sagamore. Don't ever let that bare-footed act of his fool you, kid; he's a genius. The only real, honest-to-God genius I ever saw. I've watched him operate a long time now, and he's got the touch. There ain't no use trying to develop it; you got to be born with it. Barnum couldn't have handled this thing any better than Sagamore's done it.'

'Well,' I says, 'he was a little afraid the sheriff wasn't using enough men to look for her.'

He looked at me and shook his head. 'You can say that again,' he says. 'By the way, you haven't seen the sheriff lately, have you?'

'No,' I says. 'He went back to town last night. But I reckon he'll be along pretty soon.'

'Well, he may be having a little trouble getting in here. I expect there's quite a bit of traf— Hey, you old bastard, come back here with that board.'

Murph dropped the chunk of ice and took off down the hill after Uncle Finley.

I looked around for Pop. I finally spotted him down the hill between the house and the barn, and he was really busy. The cornfield was jampacked with cars now and they was beginning to overflow up around the barn and the back of the house, so Pop was trying to direct them where to park. Most of the drivers didn't pay much attention, though. They'd just go on as far as they could, until they was up against the car ahead, and then they'd stop and everybody would jump out and head for the timber. It was an awful snarl, and I wondered how they would ever get out when they wanted to go home.

Then they started parking downhill towards the lake and around Uncle Finley's ark and filling that part up. Pop managed to keep the front yard clear and a little stretch each side of the road up the hill past where they was putting the hot-dog stand and the carnival. I backed up towards the gate, watching the rest of the space fill up. It was just like filling the neck of a bottle. He jammed 'em in on both sides of the road clear out to the trees and then solid in the road itself until the last cars was just turning in at the gate and stopping. The last two that paid was only half-way through the gate. From there back up the road as far as I could see, they was still bumper to bumper. The whole thing had stopped now, of course, so the horns started blowing. That went on for two or three minutes, and then men started jumping out and coming ahead on foot. They came through the gate, some of them, and others just climbed through the fence and headed down through the trees towards the river bottom.

I came in as Pop went over by Uncle Sagamore and leaned on the fence post and took off his hat. He mopped his face and neck with his handkerchief. 'Whew!' he says.

Uncle Sagamore put down the flour sack. It was bulging half-way to the top with money. 'Feel kind of wore out myself,' he says. He took out his tobacco and rubbed it on his overall leg and bit off a chew. 'But it looks like a man's just got to keep hustlin' night and day to keep ahead of the game, with the gov'ment takin' nearly everything he can make. Right sizeable crowd, ain't it?'

'Must be around three thousand cars,' Pop says. 'Well, there ain't no use stayin' around up here no more. You couldn't get another car in here if you greased it. Let's go meet the folks an' see if they're gettin' set up all right. The first wave of tired ones will be comin' back out of the bottom pretty soon, an' we got to be ready for 'em.'

We walked down the hill, squeezing between cars until we got to the place where the hot-dog stand was. They had it just about finished now. Anyway, they had used up all the planks. There was spaces in it here and there, and I guess that was the ones Uncle Finley had beat them to. There was a counter along the front of it. Inside they had set up the stove and icebox, and the tubs was full of pop. Murph was starting to paint a sign.

'How much do you reckon we ought to charge for hamburgers?' he asked Uncle Sagamore.

Uncle Sagamore spit and rubbed his chin with his hand. 'Well sir,' he says. 'That there's a kind of hard question to answer off-hand. Ordinarily I'd say a hamburger was worth about two bits. But on the other hand if you been walkin' around in a river bottom for five or six hours an' ain't got no lunch with you, an' then you find it's a nine-mile walk to the nearest restaurant, I reckon you wouldn't say a dollar was too much, would you?'

Murph shook his head kind of slow, and lettered the sign. 'Hamburgers $1.00.' 'Like I always say,' he says, 'you'd never think it to look at you.'

We started on down to the house, with Uncle Sagamore carrying the flour sack. The shiny house trailer was parked off to the left. A big blonde woman with a lot of bracelets and a real red mouth was standing outside the door of it. She waved at Pop.

Pop says to Uncle Sagamore, 'Come on over. I'd like to make you acquainted with Mrs. Horne. She's sort of travellin' around the country with her nieces.'

We went over. 'Hiya, boys,' Mrs. Horne says. Her hair was real smooth and shiny and about the colour of butter and it was in little waves like the grain in a piece of wood. 'I reckon this is Sagamore, and this must be Billy, huh?'

'Well sir, I'm real proud to know you,' Uncle Sagamore says. 'Sam told me about meetin' up with you last night, an' how you'd kind of worked out a dicker.'

'Dicker?' she says, and laughs. 'I was grabbed and stabbed for a flat ten per cent of the gross. You boys are really operators. But I guess it'll be worth it; I ain't seen this many men in one place since me and the girls was up at the atom project. Come on in and meet 'em. They're negative types.' She laughed again.

Pop looked at me. 'Billy, you better run on to the—'

Mrs. Horne waved a hand and her bracelets clanked. 'Oh, what the hell, let him come in. Nobody's working yet. You want him to grow up to be a sissy?'

We went in. The living-room of the trailer had long sofas on each side, and there was white slats over the windows. There was a nice rug on the floor and all along the walls there was big pictures of girls without much clothes on. A radio was playing, and two girls was sitting on one of the sofas. One had red hair and the other kind of a silvery colour, and they both was wearing romper suits like Miss Harrington's, only maybe a little skimpier. They was real pretty. You could see Pop and Uncle Sagamore thought they was nice.

Mrs Horne introduced us all. 'These is my nieces,' she says. The platinum job is Baby Collins, and the redheaded number's La Verne.'

'Hi, honey,' Baby Collins said to Pop. 'You're kind of cute in a gruesome sort of way. Wanna buy me a drink?'

'Relax, girls,' Mrs Horne says. 'These types are the Noonan boys. The customers will begin to show up later. Where's Francine?'

'In the sack,' La Verne says, and yawns. She picked up a magazine and started to look at the pictures. 'Let me know if a live one shows up.'

'I was just listening to the radio,' Mrs Horne says. 'The news is full of it. They say it's the biggest stampede since the Klondike gold rush.'

'Well sir, by golly,' Uncle Sagamore says. 'That's fine.'

'Oh, I knew it was a natural as soon as I saw those hand bills you was throwing around,' she says. 'Which one of you boys wrote that?'

'I did,' Pop says.

'Well,' she says, 'if you don't get an Oscar for it you been gypped. What time you expect the first wave of shock troops will begin to drift back from the boondocks'?

'Likely in a couple of hours,' Uncle Sagamore said. 'It's kind of hot, tiresome work, lookin' for somebody in a swamp. Especially if you got no way of knowin' if she's been found yet.'

'You got an information centre set up?' she asked.

Pop nodded. 'The carnival's got a big public address system.'

'Well,' she says, 'you boys don't miss a bet. That's all I got to say.'

We went down to the house, and Pop and Uncle Sagamore counted the money in the flour sack, and then Uncle Sagamore went off with it somewhere. The smell from the tubs was pretty bad, because there wasn't any breeze to carry it away. It was after ten o'clock now and sunny and hot. The sheriff's sound truck wasn't making any noise, and then I remembered it hadn't made any since I woke up. I wondered if the man was still asleep, but when I looked up that way he seemed to be working on the equipment, like there was something wrong with it. The whole place was real quiet except for Uncle Finley hammering away down at the ark, and the only thing that was changed was that it was just covered solid with acres and acres of cars. And then, of course, there was the carnival. But I hadn't had time to look into that yet.

I just couldn't figure out why they hadn't found Miss Harrington. Pop said that judging from the amount of money they'd took in for parking, and figuring two men to a car and allowing for the cars that was stopped back on the road, there must be between seven and eight thousand men looking for her right now. There wasn't hardly any of them up around the house and cars, either. They was all still down there looking.

Then I remember the sheriff had said he was going to be back around ten and that he wanted me to show him where we'd hid in the ferns. It was funny he hadn't come, I thought. Everybody else in this end of the state must be down there trying to find her, and he hadn't even come back. I called Sig Freed and we went down that way, skirting along the lower side of the lake. Once we got out in the timber it was just crawling with men. They was running ever which way and yelling to each other to ask if she'd been found yet. Some of them was sitting down on logs, like they was tired out already, and a few was drifting up towards the house.

It just didn't seem to make any sense, I thought. If the whole bottom was as full of men as this hillside was, they would have found a lost marble by this time. It worried me, because the only way I could figure it was that something had happened to her. Otherwise she would have heard all the racket and yelled at one of the men where she was, even if she couldn't walk any more.

It must have been nearly noon when I got back to the house. There was quite a few of the searchers up there by that time. They was up the hill from the house, mostly, on account of the smell from the tubs. Uncle Sagamore and Pop was walking around, talking to them. I asked him for a dollar to buy a hamburger.

'Murph will give you one,' he says. 'Just go on up and ask him.'

I went up to the stand. There was a big crowd of men around it now. They was complaining about the prices, but they was buying hamburgers. Everybody was asking everybody else if they'd heard whether she had been found or not. Murph and the two other men was telling them no, and making hamburgers as fast as they could. I finally squeezed through to get to the counter. Murph saw me after a while and give me a hamburger and a bottle of coke. I went across the road to see how the carnival was coming along.

There was a lot of men there too. The place was beginning to swarm with the ones coming back from the bottom. I pushed through the crowd and I could see there was five tents altogether, but there still wasn't any rides. No Ferris wheel or merry-go-round, or anything. There was this big tent in the middle, the one that had the sort of stage out in front and the sign that said, 'Girls! Girls! Girls!' The others was a shooting gallery and a toss-the-hoop, and a couple of wheels of fortune.

I was just about to go look for Pop and see if he'd give me some money for the shooting gallery, when a man got up on the stage. There was a microphone on a stand in the middle of it, and he walked over to it and whistled. The big loudspeakers on both sides of the stage went, *Wheet! Wheet!* Then five girls come out of the doorway of the tent and up the steps of the stage. They lined up behind the man. They was real pretty, and didn't have hardly anything on in the way of clothes.

'Ladies and gentlemen,' the man with the microphone started to say, but there was so much racket he had to stop.

Everybody around me was yelling. Some of 'em was shouting, 'Hooray! Bring on the girls!' and 'Shut up and let 'em dance!' But some more was yelling, 'Hey, what the hell is this? What about Choo-Choo?'

'The whole thing looks like a fake,' another man yelled.

'I bet she ain't even been here,' somebody else says.

The uproar was getting real bad now. And then suddenly Pop was up on the stage beside the man with the microphone. He eased the man out of the way and started talking.

'Men,' he says, 'I been asked to make an announcement. I'm Sam Noonan, an' it was my little boy Billy that was with Miss

125

Caroline when them gangsters attacked her. She saved his life, men.'

They kept yelling.

'The hell with that.'

'Where is she now? How come we can't find her?'

'What kind of sellout is this, anyway?'

'It's a racket.'

'Get outta the way, you jerk, so we can see the girls.'

'Shut up and let him talk. Maybe we'll find out something.'

Pop held up his hands for them to be quiet. 'Just listen for a minute and I can answer all your questions. You read in the papers and heard on the radio how they been looking for her in twenty-three states because she was a witness in a big murder in New Orleans, an' how she was hiding out right here on this farm. Of course, we didn't even know who she was until the day the gangsters got her an' opened up on her an' my son Billy.' The noise was dying down now.

Somebody yelled, 'Let him talk.'

Pop kind of gulped, like he had a catch in his throat. 'Well sir, men,' he went on. 'That there girl, Miss Choo-Choo Caroline, is lost right here on this farm somewhere – and men, she saved my son's life. I want her found, so I can thank her.' He kind of broke down then, and had to wait a minute before he could go on.

'What she done, men, was the bravest thing I ever heard of in my life. But wait a minute, everybody. Wait a minute. I see my son down there in the crowd right now, and I'm goin' to let him tell you in his own words. Billy, will you come up here? Make way there, men, and let him through.'

I gulped down the last of my hamburger and started towards the stage. Everybody moved aside to let me through. When I got to it, Pop leaned down and caught my hands to lift me up, and there I was right in front of everybody. He put an arm across my shoulders. The crowd let out a cheer.

'Now, son,' he says, pulling me over in front of the microphone and lowering it a little, 'I want you to tell everybody out there what a heroic thing that girl done, savin' your life, an' how much you think of her.'

I started out. I told 'em how we was swimming and how the water suddenly started getting chewed up all around us with that noise the guns was making on the other bank. And when I was telling how she caught me by the neck and pulled me under the water and towed us along till we was under the bushes, I looked around and doggone if Pop wasn't crying. He was trying to hold back the tears, kind of gulping like he was swallowing something too big for his throat, and then at last he had to haul out his handkerchief and dab at his eyes. When I finished up everybody was cheering and waving their hats.

'We'll find her, Billy,' they yelled.

Pop took hold of the microphone again, and had to clear his throat a couple of times before he could talk. 'There you are, men,' he says. 'That's the kind of girl Miss Choo-Choo Caroline is. Besides bein' one of the most beautiful women that ever lived, she's one of the bravest. An' now she's been lost down there in that wild river bottom for over eighteen hours without hardly a stitch of clothes on, nor nothin' but that little patch of diamond-covered ribbon half the size of your hand, with the mosquitoes bitin' her all over that lovely young body an' brambles scratchin' her on the legs, an' nothin' to keep the night chill off. We got to find her, men. We just got to find her.'

The crowd let out a big roar then. It was getting bigger all the time. Then I saw Uncle Sagamore coming up on the stage.

Pop went on. 'An' now here's my brother Sagamore, that's in charge of the search. He's been up all night without a wink of sleep, goin' back and forth acrost that bottom tryin' to find her. And he ain't goin' to give up as long as there's a breath left in his body. He knows that river bottom like you know the palm of your hand, and he'll tell you anything you want to know about it.'

Everybody cheered Uncle Sagamore. He took hold of the microphone and shifted his tobacco over into the other cheek, and says, 'Well sir, men, I ain't no hand at makin' speeches. You all know that. I'm just goin' to tell you I appreciate you comin' out to help an' all, an' I know you're going' to be just like me. You're goin' to be right here, by hell, till that there girl is found.

'Now, naturally, a man can't look all the time. We wouldn't expect him to. He's got to have a little rest now an' then, so there's refreshments up here, an' entertainment for when you get tired.'

There was a big commotion up the hill then, in that jam of cars just this side of the gate. And just as I looked, three big hound dogs came lunging through the last row of cars and into the open section of the road. They was yanking along some man that had hold of their leashes, and then they gave a big lunge and pulled him off his feet. He slid along on his stomach for maybe his own length before he could get up, and when he did and I got a look at his face, doggone if it wasn't the sheriff. He was dusty and sweaty and limping a little, and his face was purple. It looked like he was cussing the dogs or something, but they was baying and the loudspeakers was going on with Uncle Sagamore's speech, so you couldn't be sure. Behind him there was another man with three more of the big, long-eared dogs.

They come on down and hit the edge of the crowd and began pushing their way through, being more or less pulled along by the bloodhounds or whatever they was. Just as they got down in front of the stage, Uncle Sagamore looked out and saw them.

'Well sir, by golly,' he says into the microphone. 'Here's the shurf. He's come to help us. It's just like I was sayin', men, he might be a little late gettin' on the job, but I knowed he wouldn't let us down.'

The sheriff got the dogs stopped. He looked up at us on the stage and at the five naked girls behind us, and he pointed at Uncle Sagamore with his mouth open and his face as purple as a ripe plum, but you couldn't tell whether he was saying anything or not.

'I always said that shurf was a damn good man,' Uncle Sagamore went on, 'an' I tell you right now there wasn't never the slightest doubt in my mind that he'd come out here sooner or later an' help us out in our hour of need. I got to admit, though, that it does seem to me like it was kind of cheap of the shurf's office not to offer no more than a little old measly five-hundred-dollar reward for that girl. I'd be the last one in the world to find fault, but it does seem to me they could of made it at least a thousand.'

The crowd let out another big cheer.

Uncle Sagamore finished up. 'Well, I ain't goin' to stand here an' jaw at you fellers all day. You don't want to look at no homely old bastard like me, with all them pretty girls up here to dance for you. So I thank you kindly.'

He stepped away from the microphone and the man came back. 'All right, folks,' he says, 'now we'll give you a little sample of the stupendous show you'll see inside the tent. So step right up and get your tickets. Only one dollar—'

Music blared out of the loudspeaker then and we all got down off the stage so the girls could dance. It was real pretty to watch. They kicked their legs up high and wiggled all over.

Men was pushing around the little stand to buy tickets. I followed Pop and Uncle Sagamore down towards the house. The Sheriff was shoving his way through the crowd with the dogs, and I could see he was trying to catch up with us. I caught Uncle Sagamore's arm.

'I think the sheriff wants to see you,' I says.

He stopped. 'Why, sure,' he says. We was under the big tree near Mrs Horne's shiny trailer.

The sheriff come up. He handed the leashes of the three hounds to the other man to hold.

He waved his hand, sort of. 'Sagamore Noonan—' he says. He rubbed both hands across his face and tried again. 'Sagamore Noonan—' It seemed like that was as far as he could get. He was breathing real hard.

Uncle Sagamore leaned against the tree and shifted his tobacco over into his other cheek real thoughtful. 'Why, yes, Shurf,' he says. 'Did you want to talk to me?'

The sheriff says, '—*fffftt – sshhh – ffffttt—*'

It reminded me of when he tried to open the jar of tannery juice and spilled it all over his clothes. It looked like the words was all jammed up inside him and he couldn't get 'em turned lengthwise so they would come out. He reached in the pocket of his coat and brought out something. It was two things, really. One of 'em was a copy of the hand bill me and Pop had printed up, and the other was a folded newspaper. He held the newspaper out in front of Uncle Sagamore with one hand and started slapping the front of it with the other, still not saying words but just going on with that sort of wheezing. I stood on tiptoes and craned my neck a little so I could see the front of the paper. And doggone if it wasn't a real big picture of Miss Harrington. I mean Miss Caroline.

She didn't have on anything but her diamonds, but this time there was three patches of them. She was posed in front of a great big fan or something that looked like it was made out of ostrich feathers. And it seemed like the whole first page of the paper was about her. The headline said:

SOUGHT IN WILDS . . . SCANTILY CLAD DANCER
OBJECT OF FRENZIED SEARCH

I tried to read what it said, but the way the sheriff was waving it around and slapping it with his other hand I couldn't get any more than snatches of it. ' . . . *most fantastic manhunt in history* . . .

Wild confusion . . . Stampede fanned by rumours of reward . . . The already fabulous Choo-Choo Caroline, beautiful missing witness in gangland murder case . . . sweetheart of late gang leader . . . alleged to have fled almost nude into swamp . . . '

I didn't know what a lot of the big words meant, but it sure looked as if everybody was interested in her.

Uncle Sagamore took the paper out of the sheriff's hand and studied it. 'Well, sir,' he says, 'that there's a right nice picture of her, ain't it, Shurf?'

The sheriff took another deep breath. He rubbed both hands up over his face and then down again, and this time the log jam of words inside him got straightened out and he began talking. It wasn't loud, or anything. He talked real calm and low, like a man that was trying to hold his breath at the same time he was saying words. It was more like a whisper.

'Sagamore Noonan,' he says, 'if there was any way the moral law would let me, I'd pull a gun right here an' kill you. I'd shoot you, an' then I'd go runnin' up the road laughing like a hyena, an' they'd let me go. They wouldn't do a thing to me. At the very worse they'd just lace me up in a strait jacket or put me in a padded cell, an' I'd have all the rest of my life with nothing to do but just stand there with my head stuck out through the bars and laugh about never being the sheriff again of a county that had you in it.'

'Listen,' he says, still whispering. 'They got all the highway patrol cars in this end of the state out there on that road south of town, tryin' to untangle the snarl. It'll be two o'clock this afternoon before they can get any traffic across it. That's just the highway. From here out *to* the highway, there's four solid miles of abandoned cars jammed bumper to bumper in the road. They just got out and left 'em, and took the keys. You can't get round 'em, and you can't move 'em without a wrecker – or twenty wreckers. And we can't even get the wreckers to 'em until they get that highway open.

'I walked in here from two miles this side of town. That's the only way you can get in here, or out. The woods is swarming with newspaper reporters and photographers and radio news people that tried to make it on foot and got lost.'

He took another deep breath, and went on, 'There's whole towns as far as fifty miles from here that ain't got a man left in 'em. The stores are closed. The buses have stopped running. Construction jobs are deserted. Whole communities is empty except for women and the women is raving. I got relays of girls answering the phone, tryin' to tell people there ain't been any reward offered for that girl. Ain't none of 'em been able to stick it out more'n two hours. They can't stand the language.

'And now that you've turned this place into a honky tonk, I never will get 'em out of here until we find that there girl and show 'em she's been found. They wouldn't leave, even if they could get their cars out.'

Uncle Sagamore pursed up his lips like he was going to spit, only he didn't, and he rubbed his chin real thoughtful. 'Well, Shurf,' he says. 'That's what we're all tryin' to do, find that there girl. Why don't we just all pitch in together an' look for her? We been waitin' all day for you to get down here on the job an' do somethin' about tryin' to locate her.'

'You – you—' the sheriff says. He was beginning to fizz and sputter again.

'Why, shucks,' Uncle Sagamore went on. 'I don't see nothin' for us *to* do, but keep on looking. You got lots of help. An' it don't seem to me like you'd want to start raisin' no stink about the reward. You want to have all them people goin' around sayin' mebbe that shurf don't even care whether that there girl's found or not? Why, they might get real violent.'

The sheriff lunged out and caught the leashes of the other three hounds. 'Give me them dogs,' he snarled at the man. 'Let's go.' Then he looked around at me. 'Billy, you come along and show us where you hid in them ferns.'

The dogs barked. They had a real deep, rumbling sort of bark. They lunged on the leashes and almost pulled the sheriff off his feet again.

'Damn it—' he says.

And just then there was another voice behind us. We whirled around and Baby Collins was standing in the door of the trailer, leaning against the door frame with a cigarette in her hand. She was wearing a wrap-around sort of thing made out of some lacy black stuff you could see right through, with one bare leg slanting a little out of the front of it.

'Hi, honey,' she says to the sheriff. 'Why don't you tie up your dogs and come in out of the sun? We'll open a box of cornflakes.'

Sixteen

The Sheriff got a little darker red in the face, and Uncle Sagamore says to Baby Collins, 'I'd like to make you acquainted with the shurf. He's a real busy man, though.'

'Oh,' she says. 'That's too bad. But I'm glad to meet you, sheriff. Drop in and see us any time you're out this way, and bring your scrabble board.'

She smiled at all of us and went back to the trailer.

The big hounds was lunging on the leashes again, about to pull the sheriff over, and there was so much uproar when he finally was able to talk again you couldn't tell whether it was Uncle Sagamore he was cussing or the dogs. Sig Freed got mixed up in it too. He'd bark at the hounds and then run around in a circle and jump up on me, just to be sure I was still there to back him up in case they got mad. Any one of 'em could have swallowed him with one bite.

We started to go down past the house, but all of a sudden the sheriff stopped. 'Oh, hell,' he says. 'We got to have something of hers for the dawgs to get the scent.'

'That's right,' the other man says. It was the first time he'd even opened his mouth. I guess he was a new deputy. He was a kind of sandy-haired man with a long neck and weak blue eyes.

The sheriff waved an arm. 'Run up there to that trailer they was livin' in and see if you can find a pair of her shoes, or some clothes. The trailer's off there somewhere in that mess of cars.'

'Hey, wait,' I says. 'I just remember Uncle Sagamore had had some clothes of hers last night. 'Uncle Sagamore had—'

The whole thing happened so fast then it was like something blowing up in your face. I think Sig Freed was starting to leap up on me again, or was already in the air, but anyway Pop lunged and grabbed me and hoisted me up, and at the same time he cried, 'Did you see that? That dam' dawg tried to bite Billy—'

'He did?' Uncle Sagamore says. He made a lunge at Sig Freed and waved his hat at him. 'Git. Shoo! Scat, you goddam dawg!'

Everybody was excited and yelling. The sheriff says, 'What the hell?' I tried to tell Pop that Sig Freed wasn't trying to bite, that he was just playing, but his hand was over my mouth the way he was holding me, and then he was running towards the house with me on his shoulder, yelling, 'We better see if he broke the skin. Might have hydrophoby.'

He was cussing Sig Freed so loud all the time he was running I couldn't get him to understand I was all right, even if he hadn't had my face pressed against his shoulder so I couldn't talk clear. He ran up on the porch and went into the bedroom, and put me down on the bed.

'Here,' he says, all excited, pulling up my pants leg. 'Let me see where it was! Doggone that dawg! I knowed all the time you couldn't trust him.'

'Pop,' I says, 'for the love of Pete, I been trying to tell you. He didn't bite me. He didn't even try. He was just playing.'

He stared at me with his mouth open. 'Oh,' he says. He took out his handkerchief then and mopped his face. 'Whew! Sure give me a scare, anyway. You're sure you're all right!'

'Of course,' I says. I got up off the bed.

'I could have swore he nipped at you,' Pop says, like he still could believe it.

'We better get back,' I says. 'The sheriff wants me to go with him to start the dogs on the trail.'

'Sure,' he says. 'They're gone now to see if they can find something of hers for the scent.'

'That was what I was going to tell him, when you grabbed me,' I says. 'Uncle Sagamore had some of her clothes.'

'Oh,' Pop says. He frowned kind of thoughtful. 'I don't know whether I'd tell him that or not. Course, I suppose it'd be all right – No, I expect we'd better not.'

'Well?' I asked. 'What's wrong with that?'

'Well,' he says, 'she's lost, you see, and Dr Severance has been shot, so in a way everything in that trailer has been impounded by the gov'ment and nobody's supposed to touch anything until the estate has been settled. It's kind of legal stuff you wouldn't understand very well. Of course, it's all right for the shurf to go in there, but not us. Uncle Sagamore put the stuff back, of course, when he didn't find her, but it might be a good idea not to say anything about it.'

'Oh,' I says. 'Well, I won't mention it.'

We went back out. Uncle Sagamore and the sheriff had come down close to the front yard and was waiting. The smell from the tubs was pretty bad there, and the sheriff was fanning the air with his hat. In a minute the other deputy came back. He had that pair of gold sandals of Miss Harrington's – I mean Miss Caroline's.

Me and the sheriff and the deputy started down below the

lake with them holding on to the dogs' leashes. When we got around on the lower side of it in the timber there was men everywhere, still looking.

'I don't know how the hell a dawg could foller nothin' in this trampled-up mess,' the sheriff says, real bitter. 'Help! Hah! We'll be the rest of the fall roundin' up the lost hunters, after we locate her.'

We went on up through the woods until we was across from the place where we swum, and I showed the sheriff where we climbed out of the water while they was shooting at us. From there it was only a little way through the timber to the little gully with the ferns growing around it. For a wonder, there wasn't anybody else around, and the ferns hadn't been trampled on. You could still see the broken ones where we had hid.

'You see?' I says. 'Right there.'

'Good,' the sheriff says. 'I'm glad somebody around this place is a decent, intelligent, common, ordinary, co-operatin' human being. You're all right, Billy.'

Being back here on the spot reminded me of how we'd listened to the other gangsters going by in the leaves while we was hid. I told the sheriff about it. 'So there must have been three of them,' I said. 'Maybe the other one's still down here, or else he got away.'

He shook his head. 'No. He didn't get away. We found the car out there on the road last night and nabbed him when he showed up. So far he ain't said a word, so we don't know whether he got her or not, but the fact you say you heard him makes your story check out.'

'You – you reckon he shot her, Sheriff?' I asked.

He frowned, kind of thoughtful. 'No. I don't think so. I'm pretty sure she's still alive.'

'It sure looks like they'd have found her by this time,' I says.

'Yeah,' he said. 'Don't it?'

We went over to where the deputy was holding the dogs, and the sheriff let each one of them smell the pair of sandals. They whined a little and looked real interested. Then the sheriff put the sandals inside his shirt and led the dogs over close to where we had laid in the ferns. They whined some more and pulled hard to get over to it. They went *snuff! snuff! snuff!* with their noses close to the ground, and when the sheriff and the deputy unstrapped the leashes they went swarming all over the gully, eager and excited as anything, and then one of them let out this big booming bark and started down the hill swinging back and forth with his nose close to the ground and his ears flapping. The others followed him.

'They got it!' the sheriff yelled. 'They got the scent.'

They disappeared downhill in the trees. We could hear their baying and tell which way they was going, so we ran along after them. The sheriff was pretty lame from that long walk out from town, so he had a hard time keeping up. In a minute we caught sight of them again, crossing a little open space. Four other men was chasing after them then. They was pointing and yelling.

'Hey, Joe,' one of them shouted. 'Come on. Them dawgs is on the trail. They'll lead us to her.'

Two more men came charging out of the bushes and took out after the rest. More kept coming. Every time we'd catch sight of the dogs there'd be a bigger crowd after them. We began to drop behind, but we could tell by the trampling and crashing through the brush ahead that there was a whole army of them up ahead of us trying to keep up with the dogs. The uproar got further and further away, going down towards the bottom.

The sheriff had to stop and rest. He sat down on a stump and pulled out the big red handkerchief to mop his face. He sighed and shook his head. 'You just don't know what it can do to you,' he says to the deputy, real bitter and discouraged. 'I mean, waking up in the dead of night with the cold sweat on you, wondering what the hell he'll do next. And the awful part of it is even after you've found out, you ain't going to be able to pin it on him. All you can do is go around and sort of pick up the pieces. He ain't done a lick of work in forty years that I know of; he's got plenty of time to plan these things so he's two moves ahead of you all the time.

'Now you take this one. He knows perfectly well I can't order that carnival out of here – even if it could get out, which it can't because the road's clogged with abandoned cars – which he also knew would happen. He knows I can't order it out and break up this thing because it's got a permit to operate in this county. So while the whole damn state's in a uproar over a naked cooch dancer that probably ain't even down here, he's drawin' a fat rake-off from the hamburgers and dancing girls and wheels-of-fortune and the floozies, besides selling moonshine to 'em at New York prices and charging them a dollar to park their cars into a solid snarl.

'And now, you mark my words, before it's all over there'll be something else, too – like maybe a big mudhole suddenly developing in the road and when they do get the road clear everybody will get stuck and have to be pulled out at two dollars a head.'

'Sheriff,' I says, 'you mean you still don't think Miss Caroline was with me?'

He took off his hat and mopped his head again. 'I don't really know what I think any more, Billy,' he says. 'I do believe you're telling the truth, in spite of your handicap of being a member of the Noonan family. I believe she was with you, but where she is now I wouldn't even try to guess. Do you hear them dawgs?'

'Yes,' I says. 'Sounds like they're pretty far over there.'

He nodded. 'They're about two miles away, and still going across the bottom. That girl was barefooted, and she couldn't have walked three hundred yards, but before the day's over you're going to find out the dawgs has followed her trail somewhere around eighteen to twenty miles, back and forth across this bottom. There'll be three or four thousand men following 'em, and every time they double back up past the carnival a fresh bunch of tired ones will drop off the rest and pay a dollar to watch the belly dancers, and eat hamburgers that'll get smaller and smaller and have more and more oatmeal in them and will be selling for a dollar and a half by sundown. I been through all this before. Not this particular one, mind you, but with the same Sagamore Noonan touches.'

I kind of liked the sheriff, but it seemed to me like he was too excitable and he did too much griping about Uncle Sagamore. I couldn't see anything wrong with him trying to get as many people as he could down here to look for Miss Caroline. I was worried about her, and I didn't think we ought to be just sitting here when she still hadn't been found.

'Hadn't we better start after the dogs again?' I says. 'They're still barking like they're on the trail, and they'll have to catch up with her sooner or later.'

'You don't have to follow bloodhounds that close,' he says. 'You just listen to see which way they're going. I think they're beginning to swing now, so they'll be back up this way before long. My guess is they'll go through the edge of that cornfield up there behind the house.'

Well, we waited. And sure enough, it wasn't but about half an hour before we could hear them and the whole army of men that was following them go crashing through the underbrush and timber about a furlong off to the right of us. We went over there just in time to get a glimpse of the dogs, and then we was running along in a swarm of men. The dogs went on up the hill and then, by golly, it was just like the sheriff had said. They cut along the edge of the cornfield, down back of the barn, and then headed out across the bottom again.

The sheriff looked furious, but him and the deputy started back down that way. Several hundred of the other men didn't, though. They broke away and started up through the cars in the cornfield, headed for the carnival and the hot-dog stand. I was hungry too, so I called Sig Freed and we went along behind them.

There was a terrific crowd up by the stand now, and you couldn't hardly get near the carnival. The loudspeakers was blaring and the five girls was dancing on the stage. All the other tents had big swarms around them too. Everywhere you looked there was men.

Murph and his two men was so tired they could hardly move. Murph handed me a hamburger when I finally got up close to the counter. Sure enough, the meat in it was a lot smaller than the one I'd got at noon.

'That'll-be-a-dollar-fifty-no-they-haven't-found-her,' he says.

'Pop'll pay you,' I told him.

He looked at me. 'Oh,' he says. 'I'm getting punchy, kid. I didn't even recognise you.'

I didn't see Pop and Uncle Sagamore anywhere, but there was so many men around it would be hard to see them. I tried to watch the girls dancing, but everywhere I stood there was a bunch of tall men in front of me craning to see, theirselves, and anyway they went back inside the tent in a few minutes and the people started buying tickets for the inside show. I tried to get one too, and told the man Pop would pay him.

'Kid,' he says, 'come back in fifteen years with a dollar, and I'll let you in. It's a promise.' He looked tired too, and his voice was hoarse.

I started to turn away, and then he tossed me fifty cents. 'Here, kid,' he says. 'Go over to the shooting gallery and shoot a round.'

I finally managed to squeeze my way in there, and I shot fifty cents' worth at the little targets travelling across the back of the gallery on a moving belt. I didn't hit much. When the money was gone I started looking for Pop and Uncle Sagamore. They didn't seem to be up here anywhere, so I went down to the house. The smell from the tubs hit me in the front yard, as bad as ever, or worse, and that reminded me we never had bottled up any more of the juice to send to the government to have analysed. Well, maybe, we'd get around to it when Miss Caroline was found and all this uproar died down.

That made me wonder if we *would* find her. There just wasn't any use kidding ourselves any longer; she had been lost nearly twenty-four hours now, and it looked more and more all the time like something bad had happened to her. Maybe that last gangster had shot her and put her body in one of the sloughs down there. That made me feel sick, and I was about ready to cry when I went in the house.

Pop and Uncle Sagamore was there in the front bedroom with the door closed, counting another bunch of money out of a flour sack. It was all over the bed.

'They haven't found her yet, Pop,' I says.

He nodded. 'I know. But they will; you just wait. Hell they can't help it – look at how many of them there is looking.'

'I know. Something must have happened to her.'

He slapped me on the back. 'No sir, you just buck up. I got a feeling Miss Caroline's perfectly all right.'

Uncle Sagamore took the sack of money after it was all counted and went out with it somewhere. When he came back we went out on the front porch. We could see Uncle Finley down there on top of the ark, hammering away to beat the band.

'He must figure the rain's already started,' Pop says. 'All these cars showing up around here.'

'I reckon so,' Uncle Sagamore says. 'Oh. There's Harm. I got to talk to him a minute.'

He went up beyond the front yard a little and caught up with a tall skinny man wearing khaki pants and shirt and no hat. He had a bald spot almost like Uncle Sagamore's. They talked together for a few minutes and then Uncle Sagamore came back and sat down.

It was nearly sundown now, and up there in the big swarm of men around the carnival they was hanging some electric lights on tree limbs and over the stage in front of the girl tent. I guess there was a generator on one of the trucks.

Just then the sheriff and the new deputy and Booger came around the corner of the house. They was really beat down. Booger had red rims around his eyes and a stubble of beard, and his clothes was dusty and sweat-stained. The sheriff was limping and his clothes was in about as bad a shape as Booger's.

'Set and rest a spell, men,' Uncle Sagamore says. 'You look

kind of done in. Any luck yet?'

Booger and the new deputy sat down, just kind of collapsing on the steps. The sheriff stood there, swaying a little on his feet and staring real cold at Uncle Sagamore.

'No luck yet,' he says. 'But we expect to find her any minute now. The dawgs is making their fourth trip across the bottom, hot on her trail. As near as I can figger, that adds up to around seventeen miles. She was barefooted and hadn't even been off pavement before in her life, so it stands to reason she couldn't be very far ahead of 'em now.'

Uncle Sagamore scratched his leg with his toenail. 'Well sir, it would sure seem like it.'

The sheriff nodded. 'Unless, of course, she's stretched out into a real hard run. You got to take that into consideration; she's only been going for twenty-four hours. And after she wore off the tender part of her feet, say up about half-way to her knees, they might quit bothering her and she could make better time.'

Uncle Sagamore nodded too, with his lips pursed up. 'She sure is a puzzling thing, all right, Shurf. For the life of me I just can't figger it out.'

The sheriff exploded then. He stuck a finger right in Uncle Sagamore's face and yelled, with his face purple, '*Sagamore Noonan! Where is that girl?*'

Uncle Sagamore looked at him in surprise. 'Why, Shurf, how would I know? Ain't I been lookin' for her myself practically night and day?'

Before the sheriff could say anything else, somebody called him from up near the edge of the crowd. We all looked up that way, and it was Otis. He came limping down through the yard, and he looked about as done in as the others. His eyes was red like he hadn't had any sleep, and he hadn't shaved.

The sheriff rubbed his hands across his face and says to Otis, 'How's it going out there?'

Otis kind of collapsed on the steps too. 'Well,' he says, 'they got the highway clear, with road blocks set up so no more hunters can get through to clog it up again. There's three wreckers and a bulldozer workin' on the road now, movin' the cars out of it where they can an' dozin' a path around where they can't. They're half-way in from the highway, and likely the whole road'll be open by midnight. Somebody run over the last one of Marvin Jimerson's hawgs, though, just a while ago, and he's filed suit against the county.'

'How's things in town?' the sheriff asked.

Otis shook his head. 'About the same. Women is picketing the courthouse. The PTA, the Women's Club, and the League of Women Voters held a combined mass meetin' in the high school and they're goin' to wire the governor to send the National Guard if you don't get these men out of here by mornin'. A few of the reporters has found their way back to town on foot, and word's got out about the belly dancers and the carnival and the girls, so there was some talk at the meetin' of charterin' a helicopter to bring a delegation out here, but there wasn't enough money in the treasuries.

'The road blocks is going to try to hold back the car-loads of women as soon as word comes through the road's clear into here, but they won't be able to hold 'em long if there ain't some signs of this breakin' up by morning'. And if them women get in here I'm sailin' right out across that bottom on foot and I ain't goin' to stop this side of the West Coast.'

The sheriff shuddered. 'Well, men, you got any ideas for gettin' 'em out of here? If we tell 'em that, most of 'em will be afraid to go home. They'll figure that since they're goin' to be in the dawg-house anyway they might as well live her up as long as they can. There ain't no hope of findin' that girl so we can convince 'em it's all over. She ain't down there in that bottom—' He stopped then and his eyes got real hard. Then he went on, looking at Uncle Sagamore.

'But maybe if I could make 'em understand they been horns-woggled by this crooked old wart hog here, and gypped into spendin' their money and getting theirselves in the dawghouse with their wives—'

'You reckon you could make 'em see it?' Booger asked, showing a little interest for the first time.

'I can sure try,' the sheriff says. 'They sure must be beginning to wonder theirselves why a whole army of men ain't been able to find a girl in a place that size.'

'But, look,' Otis says, with a real nasty smile. 'We couldn't do that. Why, they might lynch him.'

'Oh, of course not,' the sheriff says. 'Hell, how could they? There's four law officers here to protect him, and only about eight thousand of them.'

Seventeen

Uncle Sagamore pursed up his lips. 'Why, Shurf,' he says. 'You wouldn't do a thing like that.'

'Wouldn't I?' the sheriff says. 'But don't you worry. It's our duty as law officers to protect you. And likely there ain't more'n a few hundred of 'em got guns in their cars.'

'Hey, wait a minute.' It was Otis. 'I was just by the sound truck. It's broke down.'

The sheriff nodded. 'I know. While Rutherford was asleep last night a bunch of the wires inside his amplifier pulled themselves loose an' run off. But I'll commandeer the one up at the carnival. By God, we'll break this thing up!'

He turned around and started up towards the crowd. The deputies followed him. Pop and Uncle Sagamore looked at each other. I began to get scared. A lot of these men had been acting like they was drinking, and there was no telling what would happen.

Uncle Sagamore spit out some tobacco juice and rubbed his chin. 'Sure is a hard-workin' man, that shurf. It's a downright shame, though, he's got such a habit of goin' off half-cocked.'

He got up and sauntered along after them. Pop went with him.

There wasn't anything else for me to do, so I followed them. But I didn't like the looks of it.

When I got up there Uncle Sagamore was standing at the back of the crowd, but I didn't see Pop anywhere. When I come up behind the swarm of men I couldn't even see the stage, so I backed off across the road by the hamburger stand. That wasn't much better. I was still too low.

'What's the matter, kid?' Murph asked.

'I was trying to see the stage,' I says. 'The sheriff is going to make a speech.'

'Oh-oh,' he says. 'Well, here,' He lifted me up on the counter and we watched together. Everybody else had left to join the crowd across the road.

'I been afraid of this,' Murph said. 'There's a lot of mutterin' already.'

The girls had been dancing awful tired, as if they couldn't hardly pick up their feet any more. Then the music stopped and they staggered down the steps and into the tent. The man started over to take hold of the microphone. And then the sheriff climbed up on the stage. The man started to wave him off, but the sheriff said something we couldn't hear, and showed the man something he took out of his pocket. The man scratched his head and looked like he didn't know what to do, but then he backed away and let the sheriff have the microphone.

Now that he was over in front of it you could hear him, because it was coming out of the loudspeakers. 'Men,' he says, 'I got an announcement to make.'

Men in the crowd start to whistle and yell.

'Get down, you old fossil!'

'Who the hell wants to look at you?'

'Bring back them luscious peaches.'

'Throw the old bastard out! We want girls.'

The sheriff held up his hands and kept talking, trying to drown them out. 'Men, you're bein' made suckers of. You been gypped. Choo-Choo Caroline ain't down there in that bottom. You ought to know that by now.'

'Throw him out,' somebody yelled. 'We want girls.'

'Shut up!' somebody else shouted. 'Let him talk.'

'Yeah. He may be right.'

'How about that?'

The sheriff went on, 'There's been eight thousand of you, or maybe more, tramplin' over that bottom for ten hours. There ain't a square yard of it that ain't been walked on. If she's down there, how come you haven't found her?'

'I think he's got something there,' one of the men called out.

'You're damn right he has.'

The sheriff held up his hands again. 'All right. Let me talk. You ain't heard half of it yet. There ain't no reward offered for that girl, and never has been. You're a bunch of suckers.'

Then Pop was climbing up on the stand.

'He'd better look out,' Murph says, real soft.

Pop was holding up his hands, and talking, but you couldn't hear a word he was saying because the sheriff was drowning him out with the loudspeakers. Then a rock flew through the air, and it just missed Pop's head.

'We'll see who's a sucker!' a man yelled in the crowd.

Another rock went sailing past Pop.

'Murder!' Murph whispered. 'Me for the timber.' He looked like he was ready to start running.

But just then there was a big commotion at the back of the

crowd, on the downhill side, towards the house. A man was running this way, yelling at the top of his voice and waving something over his head. He broke into the crowd and started shoving his way through like a crazy man. When he got to the front he jumped up on the stage, still waving this thing over his head. Pop looked at it.

Then he jumped and grabbed it out of the man's hand and leaped for the microphone. The sheriff just stared, with his mouth open.

'It's the G-string!' Pop yelled into the microphone. He held it up so everybody could see it. 'The diamond G-string Choo-Choo was wearin'!'

The crowd let out a roar.

Pop grabbed the man by the arm and dragged him in front of the microphone. They jostled the poor sheriff right out of the way.

'Where'd you find it?' Pop asked. 'Tell us where you found this thing! Did you see her? Where is she?'

The man shook his head. He was all out of breath. Then I took a good look at him, and I saw it was Harm, the one Uncle Sagamore had talked to a while ago. He gasped for breath, and then he says, 'Right – down below the lake – about half a mile. It was caught – on a bush.'

The crowd roared again.

Pop held up his hands. 'There you are, men! She ain't down there, is she? That pore, lost, terrified girl! And now she ain't got a single stitch on!'

I looked down at Murph. He was leaning on the counter with his face down on his arms. When he straightened up he shook his head with a sort of dazed look in his eyes.

'Kid,' he says, 'when you grow up, just remember it was Murph that told you first.'

'Told me what?' I asked.

'That he's a genius. The only real, live genius I ever saw.'

The crowd was beginning to drown Pop out now. 'We'll find her,' they was yelling.

Pop held up his hand for silence. The other hand was still waving the diamond thing. ' . . . completely naked,' he was saying. ' . . . nothing at all to protect her from the chill. And as for the reward – Listen, men! If the shurf's office is going to try to weasel out of it, we'll pay the reward ourself! Me an' Sagamore will pay it. And not no measly five hundred dollars, neither. One thousand dollars to the man who finds that girl that saved my little boy's life.'

The crowd let out another big cheer. 'Send that useless shurf home! We'll find that girl without him.'

Uncle Sagamore came up on the stage then. They give him a cheer. 'Men,' he says into the microphone, 'I'm real proud to know you're with us right to the end. And don't feel too harsh against the shurf because he don't want to bother to look for her an' because he's too cheap to pay the reward. Remember, he's got other duties, like foreclosin' mortgages, and arrestin' people for crimes like shootin' craps or takin' a drink now and then, an' he can't spend a lot of time lookin' around in a river bottom for a young girl just because she's lost with no clothes on an' so terrified she'll probably throw herself right in the arms of the first man that finds her. Politicians is got a lot of other important things on their minds, and besides this girl can't vote, nohow. She's too young.'

There was another big roar from the crowd.

Uncle Sagamore went on, 'Now, the daylight's a-fadin' out fast, an' there ain't no point in anybody goin' back down there in the bottom now except the one's that's got flashlights and lanterns, but you stick around here until morning an' we'll find her. Somebody'll get that thousand dollars. You can get a little sleep in your cars, an' there's refreshments an' entertainment for all. I thank you kindly, men.'

I didn't even see the sheriff on the stage now. He had left.

Uncle Sagamore got down, and the poor tired girls struggled back up on the stage once more. As the music started blaring again I saw Pop and Uncle Sagamore going down towards the house. I ran and caught up with them just as they got in the front yard.

And then the sheriff and all three of the deputies came charging down on us as fast as they could walk. We sat down on the porch and they stopped in front of us. I had seen the sheriff mad lots of times before, but never like this. He pulled out his gun.

But he was only handing it to Booger. 'Hold onto it,' he says, with his voice so tight you could hardly hear him. 'Don't let me have it. I don't trust myself. I ain't never shot down an unarmed man in cold blood, and I don't want it on my soul.'

Uncle Sagamore shifted his tobacco over into the other cheek and rubbed his bare feet together. He reached down and popped the knuckles in his big toe. 'Why, shucks, Shurf,' he says. 'Ain't no call to get all het up.'

'Billy,' the sheriff says to me painfully, ignoring Uncle Sagamore, 'you're the only one I can get any truth out of. Was she in that car when they left here last night to scatter those hand bills?'

I didn't know what he was driving at. 'No,' I said. 'Of course not. How could she be? She was already lost then.'

He shook his head. 'All right,' he says to the deputies. 'They didn't take her away, and she couldn't go anywhere afoot, so she's still on this place somewhere. Let's go. And you too, Sagamore. We're going to search this place without no warrant. You want to make trouble?'

'Why, of course not, Shurf,' Uncle Sagamore says. 'You know I'm always downright anxious to co-operate with the law.'

He got up.

I went along, too. They searched everything. They went all through the house. They looked under the beds and in the closets. They looked through the barn and the corncrib and the hayloft up above it, and in the truck shed and an old tool shed that was down below the barn, and in Dr Severance's trailer.

It was full dark by then and they was using flashlights. At last there wasn't anything left but the ark. We all went down there. Uncle Finley had a lighted lantern hanging up on a plank and he was nailing away to beat the band, up on his scaffold. It was new boards he was using, too, so I guessed he was still tearing down the hamburger stand.

He saw us coming and sat down on the scaffold and pointed the hammer at us. 'No sir,' he says. 'Not a one of you! I been tryin' to make you listen for years, but you wouldn't. And now that it's here, you want to change your tune, well—'

The lantern light was glinting on his bald head. He started to laugh, waving the hammer around to point at all the cars.

'You see 'em? They come from miles. Thousands of 'em. Look at 'em. You know why? Because the rain's started, that's why. All over the world it's rainin' like pourin' water out of a boot, an' the water's risin', so they want to get aboard. Well, they'll all drowned every goddam one of 'em, because they wouldn't listen to me. Ain't no use you askin'. You're wastin' your time. And mine too. I got to have this thing finished by daylight. You can all go to hell.'

He turned around and started hammering again.

The sheriff just sighed and shook his head, and started shooting his flashlight beam in through the holes in the ark's side. He and the deputies went over it from top to bottom.

She wasn't in it. I couldn't see any reason why he thought she would be, but a lot of it I didn't understand by now anyway.

We walked back up by the house.

Pop and Uncle Sagamore sat down on the porch. The sheriff and his deputies just stood there. The smell from the tubs was bad, but everybody was too tired and had too much on his mind to notice it any more.

'Shurf,' Uncle Sagamore says, real sad, 'this kind of mistrust hurts my feelin's, but I ain't one to hold a grudge.'

The sheriff just looked at him. He was too beat to get mad any more. He turned to Booger.

'Boys,' he says, 'we're whipped. There's only one other slim chance. She might be in one of them cars out—'

'Oh, no,' Booger says.

'Oh, no,' Otis says.

The other deputy didn't say anything. He didn't seem to be much of a talker.

The sheriff sighed. 'I know. There's at least three thousand of 'em. It'll take till daylight, and every one of us is dead on his feet. But it's all we got left. And if we don't break this thing before sunrise, hell is going to look like a rest home. We'll have the National Guard in here, or we'll have them women and be wishin' we *did* have the National Guard – or the Marines.'

Booger shuddered. Otis shuddered. The other deputy started to, but then decided it would take too much effort. He just rolled a cigarette.

'All right,' they says. They turned on their flashlights and started down towards the lower end of the cornfield. I walked over to where I could see them. It looked like a waste of time to me. If she was in one of those cars she'd have been able to find her way back by herself. The lights was like fireflies way down there as they walked along real slow, shining them in the cars and looking in, one by one. I thought of the acres and acres of cars all over the place and was sure glad I wasn't a sheriff or a deputy.

Pop and Uncle Sagamore went up the hill towards the carnival; I just stayed there on the porch with Sig Freed. I didn't even want a hamburger. I was awful tired, and I was scared, thinking about Miss Harrington – I mean Miss Caroline. After a while they came back, carrying some more money in a sack, and a lantern. Mrs Horne was with them. She looked tired too.

'God,' she says, 'I never saw anything like it. It's like Dago with the fleet in.'

They went inside the house. After a while I got up to get away from the smell of the tubs and walked down a little way towards Uncle Finley's ark, to where there was a little open space between all the parked cars and I could look out over the lake. It was nice down there, with all the stars shining overhead and the loud-speaker music just far enough away to be pretty. I laid down, still worrying about why we couldn't find her.

When I woke up a flashlight was shining in my face.

'Hey, Billy, you oughtn't to be asleep on the ground like that,' the sheriff's voice said.

I sat up and rubbed my eyes. Sig Freed was still there beside me. 'What time is it?' I asked.

'About two in the morning.' His voice sounded like he was ready to go to sleep on his feet. 'You better go up and get in your bed.' He went on shining his light in cars.

I walked up to the house. There was a lamp burning in the front room, but Pop and Uncle Sagamore wasn't anywhere around. So I went up to the stand to see if I could get a hamburger. The generator was still running, so there was lights, but the music had stopped and there wasn't any sign of the girls. The other tents was closed too. A few men was sitting around, but it looked like most of the crowd had decided to go to sleep till morning.

There was only one plank left of the hamburger stand. Murph was sitting on top of the icebox smoking a cigarette and watching Uncle Finley knock that one loose with his hammer. He looked beat too. Uncle Finley put the plank under his arm and went down the hill in the dark.

Murph watched him go, and then he sighed and shook his head. 'God, what a day.'

'Have you got a hamburger?' I asked.

'Just one,' he says. He got up and opened the icebox and took it out. It was already cooked and in the bun. 'I been saving it for you.'

'Thanks, Murph,' I says. I started eating it. 'Have you seen Pop and Uncle Sagamore?'

He shook his head. 'Not since before midnight.'

That was funny, I thought. I wondered where they could have gone. I went back down to the house, still eating the hamburger, and looked again, but they wasn't there anywhere. I came back and sat down on the porch. They had just disappeared, that funny way they had of doing sometimes, in broad daylight. While I was sitting there somebody else came down through the yard and I could see it was a girl. It was La Verne.

'Have you seen Mrs Horne?' she asked me. 'Or Baby Collins?'

I told her about Mrs Horne being with Pop and Uncle Saga-more earlier in the night. 'I can't find them, either,' I said.

'That's funny,' she says. 'They've been gone for hours.'

She went back to the trailer. I went off up the hill to look some more. They just wasn't anywhere. After a couple of hours of poking around every place I could think of, I began to get scared. Miss Caroline was gone, and now Pop and Uncle Sagamore. I didn't have anybody.

I went down to the barn, and then back to the house again, and then up the hill where the sheriff was still looking in the last bunch of cars. He hadn't seen them either, not for hours.

There was a little red in the east now.

I heard a commotion up by the gate, and when I went up there a bulldozer was pushing down small trees on the other side of the road, and a couple of wreckers was dragging cars around. They had the road cleared out now. But where was Pop and Uncle Sagamore?

I started back down the hill, and just after I got past where Murph was asleep on his icebox I happened to look at the top of the house and saw smoke was coming out of the stovepipe. They'd come back and was frying the baloney for breakfast! I started to run, and when I was going through the yard I almost crashed into Uncle Finley, coming around the corner of the house carrying a plank.

I ran on past him and into the house.

They wasn't there. There was nobody in the kitchen, and no baloney frying. The stove was cold. I lifted one of the lids and felt the ashes. They was cold too. Maybe I was going crazy. I stuck my head out the back door and looked up. There was the smoke all right, coming up out of the stovepipe. It was just like it had been that first day we got here – smoke coming up out of cold ashes.

I was too tired and too worried about Pop and Uncle Sagamore to puzzle over it. I went back out on the front porch and sat down on the step. In a few minutes Uncle Finley came up the hill and went around back of the house. There came a sound like nails being pulled, and then he hurried back through the yard with another board, headed for the ark. He sure figured the flood was going to hit here about sunrise, I thought. It was an odd-looking board, and I wondered where he was getting them now. It didn't seem to make much difference, though.

The sheriff came down the hill looking like an old, old man. He sat down on the step and took off his hat and just looked down at his feet. He was whipped.

'Pop and Sagamore have just disappeared,' I told him.

He didn't act like he even heard me.

'Well, this is the end of everything,' he says. 'I'm finished. When they have to send in help to handle something I couldn't take care of myself—' He stopped and shook his head.

I could hear the wreckers moving the cars up by the gate, and then I saw Booger and Otis and the other deputy coming down the hill. It was full daylight.

The sheriff got up kind of slow and hopeless and walked around the side of the house, like he wanted to be alone and didn't want his deputies to see him beaten down like that. Booger and Otis came on down through the yard and just collapsed on the steps. Nobody said anything.

Then, all of a sudden, the sheriff came flying back around in front of the house. I couldn't hardly believe it was the same man. He was just scooting over the ground. Tears was running down his cheeks and he was making a funny sound way down in his throat.

Otis and Booger sprung up. 'What is it?' they asked.

'. . . *wug – wug – wug*—,' the sheriff says. He plucked at Booger's and Otis's sleeves and then backed away from them a little, pointing towards the house with the other arm.

His mouth worked, but nothing came out except '. . . fffftttt – sssssshhhhhh—' It looked like he was laughing, or maybe strangling, and those great big tears kept rolling down his cheeks.

He pulled at their sleeves again and ran a little way ahead of them, like a dog trying to get someone to follow him. He was gasping for breath and I knew he was trying to say something, but the words just wouldn't come out.

Booger and Otis looked at each other. Then Otis shook his head and looked down at the ground, 'Damn it,' he says, like he was about to cry hisself, 'what could you expect, with all he's been through?'

The sheriff's upper plate fell out and he stepped on it. He put it back in upside down and tried to close his mouth over it. He stepped up real close to Booger and put his left hand on Booger's shoulder, still holding the right one out to point at the house. It looked like he wanted to dance. Booger started to take a few steps with him, probably figuring it would be better not to get him angry.

'Gwufff,' the sheriff says. He broke away from Booger and ran back around the side of the house.

'We better get them teeth away from him before he bites hisself,' Otis says.

Booger frowned. 'No. I think he wants us to follow him.'

Sure, that was it. That was what he'd wanted all along, only he just couldn't say anything. We ran around the house past the tubs, and into the back yard. And there he was.

He was on his knees in the dirt with his hands clasped together down in front of him, looking at the rear wall of the house, or what should have been the rear wall. He was crying like a baby.

I looked. And I never saw anything like it in my life.

Eighteen

It was like a stage.

Uncle Finley had pulled about ten or twelve planks off the back of the house, and had opened up one whole side of a hidden room nobody had ever known was there. It was about three feet wide and ran the full length of that back bedroom, from the kitchen wall to this end of the house. There was no doors in it, and no windows, but there was a trap door in the floor. That was closed.

And there was Pop. And Uncle Sagamore. And Mrs Horne. And Baby Collins. And Choo-Choo Caroline.

They was all sound asleep, sitting on the floor with their backs against the other wall, facing out this way. There was a lantern, still burning, hanging from a nail in the wall above their heads. It looked funny, burning that way in broad daylight. Uncle Sagamore was in the middle. Mrs Horne and Baby Collins had their heads dropped on his shoulders. And Pop and Miss Caroline was on the outside, their heads resting on Mrs Horne's and Baby Collins's shoulders. Baby Collins was wearing her romper suit, and Miss Caroline had on one of Uncle Sagamore's shirts and a pair of his overalls with the legs rolled up. There was three empty fruit jars on the floor in front of them.

There was three tubs full of something way over at the left end, and at the right end of the little room there was some funny kind of apparatus I'd never seen before. It looked a little like a boiler, and it had a firebox under it with a little fire still burning in it. A piece of copper pipe come out the top of it and then bent over and went down, sort of coiled up, into a steel barrel that was full of water. There was just a short piece of it sticking out of the side of the water barrel down near the bottom, bent over a little, like a spigot. There was a thin sliver of wood stuck up into the spigot, and something was dripping off the end of it into a fruit jar that was full and overflowing onto the floor.

I stared at the stovepipe that came up from the firebox under the boiler. It bent and went out over the ceiling of the kitchen. So that was the reason for the smoke coming out when there was no fire in the cookstove. They both used the same stovepipe.

I looked around at Booger and Otis and the sheriff. The sheriff was still down on his knees. He wiped the tears out of his eyes with his sleeves, and started to laugh. Then he was crying again. Booger and Otis was just standing there, shaking hands. Booger went over and stuck a finger into the jar of stuff under the spigot and tasted it. He looked at the other two and nodded, smiling from one ear to the other. Then he came back and him and Otis shook hands some more. Otis went over and got two of the six or eight jars that was sitting on the floor near the one that was overflowing. They had caps on them. He uncapped them, one at a time, and tasted the stuff that was inside. Then he nodded real solemn to Booger, and they shook hands again. Then they put their hands on each other's shoulders and danced a jig. I never saw such crazy people.

'Gwufff,' the sheriff said. He was pointing at the tubs, and at the boiler, and at the stovepipe.

Booger and Otis reached down and took out his upper plate and turned it around and popped it back into his mouth. He didn't even seem to notice. But when he tried to talk now, words came out.

'Boys,' he says. 'Boys—' He broke down then, and started the crying and laughing stuff again.

'Those stinking tanner tubs was to keep us from smelling the mash,' Booger said. 'And the smoke – well, who pays any attention to smoke coming out of a kitchen stovepipe? And that's the reason he brought Choo-Choo Caroline in here. He knew the dawgs couldn't get her scent over that tannery smell. It was the only safe place to hide her until he'd milked those searchers for all the money they had. And look—' he pointed at the steel water barrel – 'you see he's got gravity flow water coming in there all the time, probably from a spring somewhere up the hill. And the outflow goes down into the lake.'

So that was the funny warm spot in the lake, I thought. And of course it was there only when this apparatus was working. I looked to see why I'd never seen the pipes under the house when I was playing around with Sig Freed, and darned if they didn't go down right through one of the blocks the foundation timbers was sitting on. It was really clever.

'What is it?' I asked Booger.

'A still,' he says. 'For making moonshine.'

The sheriff had stopped laughing and crying now, and had got up and was just standing there kind of quiet, like a man in church. 'Boys,' he says, sort of whispering, 'I don't think you've seen the real beauty of this thing yet. Now, listen.

'What I want you to do is go out there and round up that whole crowd. All eight thousand of 'em. Use the public address system, and don't let anybody get away. Make 'em all come over here and see this. They can come around that side of the house, pass along here, and go back around the corner. Every man in the county is out here, so besides the still and the mash and the moonshine, we're going to have eight thousand eyewitnesses.'

Booger frowned. And then he says, 'But, wait. You can't do that. You'll have plenty of witnesses, but you won't never be able to have a jury, because they'll be disqualified.'

The sheriff shook his head, real gentle. 'Boys, I told you you didn't see the real beauty of it. Sure, all the men are out here. But how about the women?'

Booger's and Otis's jaw fell open.

I thought the sheriff was going to break down and cry again. He started to choke up, and tears was running down his cheeks, but he was smiling. 'You see, boys? You see? There won't be nobody eligible for jury duty but them women. The ones that would lynch him if they could get their hands on him right now. The wives of the men he's been selling rotgut to and cleanin' out in crap games for twenty years.'

Booger and Otis stared at him like Uncle Finley seeing the Vision. 'I never heard anything as beautiful in my life,' Booger says, real soft.

The sheriff nodded. 'All right, boys. Round 'em up. But do me a little favour, first. Give me ten minutes here, completely alone. I'm getting along in years, and I won't never have another moment like this. I just wánt to stand here and look at him settin' there asleep between his mash tubs and his still. It'll be something to take into my old age with me.'

They left.

I was worried. 'What will they do to Pop?' I asked the sheriff. 'And to Miss Caroline?'

He didn't act like he even heard me. He just stood there with that dreamy expression on his face, and every once in a while he would whisper, 'Wonderful.' And then, 'Beautiful, beautiful, beautiful.'

It was maybe five minutes before he looked around and even noticed I was there, and then I thought of one other thing that still puzzled me. Uncle Sagamore had got some clothes for Miss Caroline, but there she was wearing his old overalls. I asked the sheriff about it.

'Oh,' he says. 'Those clothes of hers was what the dawgs was following back and forth across the bottom yesterday. He drug 'em along the ground behind his mule. I knew that, but I just figured it was a pair of her shoes.'

In a few minutes men began to come pouring down the hill. The whole back yard was full of them. The road was open now, and the first thing to get through was three car-loads of newspaper reporters and photographers. They asked a thousand questions and snapped pictures. Everybody milled around, talking, and Pop and Uncle Sagamore and the three women slept right on like babies.

Booger shook his head. 'It must have been some party,' he said. 'At least a couple of gallons.'

There was a loud honking then, and a truck come around the house and began pushing up through the crowd. It stopped right under the chinaberry tree, and I saw it had a bunch of planks on it and that the sign on the side said, 'E. M. Staggers Lumber Co.' There was a big, pleasant-faced woman wearing a sunbonnet in the seat beside the driver. She got out and walked over and stood looking at all five of them still asleep. Then she looked at me.

'Billy?' she asked.

'Yes, ma'am,' I said.

Tears came in her eyes, and she grabbed me. 'You poor boy.'

She picked me up and held me with my face pressed against her bosom.

'Get 'em out of here, sheriff,' she says. 'Get 'em off this farm. This minute.'

'Yes, Miss Bessie,' the sheriff says. 'They're on their way right now.'

I stayed on at the farm with Aunt Bessie, and it was real nice except for being a little quiet now that Pop and Uncle Sagamore was gone. I went fishing a lot, and practised swimming in the shallow water, and helped Aunt Bessie pick blackberries. She was real nice, and I liked her. Of course I missed Miss Harrington – I mean Miss Caroline – but I got a letter from her and she said she was doing fine. After she testified in the trial in New Orleans she got a job dancing in a nightclub in New York.

Well, that was in June, when they drafted Pop and Uncle Sagamore, and then about the end of August a funny thing happened. Me and Aunt Bessie was sitting on the front porch in the afternoon taking the shells off some beans when one of the sheriff's cars come bucking and bouncing down the hill with a big cloud of dust boiling up behind it. For a minute it reminded me of the old days, and I was kind of lonesome for Pop and Uncle Sagamore, thinking about how it had always been so exciting with them around. But it wasn't Booger and Otis in the car. It was the sheriff hisself.

The car slid to a stop and he got out and run up to the steps, where Aunt Bessie was watching him like he'd gone crazy.

'They're comin' back!' he yells. He took his hat off and started mashing it up in his hands. 'They'll be here tomorrow—'

Aunt Bessie dropped all the beans out of her lap. 'What!' she says. 'How did that happen? I thought—'

I jumped up. 'Hooray!' I said.

The sheriff glared at me like he wanted to bite my head off. Then he kind of collapsed on the steps and shook his head.

'The Governor pardoned 'em both,' he says, real hopeless and bitter. 'Said they didn't have a fair trial because I disqualified all the men on the jury panel and all the women was prejudiced.'

Aunt Bessie nodded her head. 'I reckon that was a mistake.'

The sheriff threw his hat out in the yard and started to say a bad cuss word. He choked it off just in time. 'No, no, no!' he says. 'That ain't it at all. That's just the *excuse*.'

Aunt Bessie looked at him. 'How's that?'

'It's that warden, dad-gum it all! He ain't never liked me, and he's the Governor's brother-in-law. The two of 'em cooked it up so they could get rid of him and throw him back on me.'

'You mean the warden didn't want him up there?' she asked.

The sheriff turned his head and stared at her. 'Bessie, how long you been married to him?'

She sighed. 'I reckon it was kind of a foolish question.'

'There ain't no doubt of it,' the sheriff says. 'That dad-gummed warden just got tired of havin' his prison in a uproar all the time, and he was jealous because the two of 'em was making more money than he was, what with the still they set up in the boiler room to make moonshine out of dried prunes and potato peelings from the kitchen, and what with the horse-race bets. And then they sold the Bramer bulls from the prison rodeo to some dog food cannery – ain't nobody ever figured out how they smuggled them out. Course, the sheet metal from the licence plate shop was easy. They used the warden's car for that . . .'

Oh, that was a fine summer, all right. Like Pop says, there ain't nothing like wholesome farm life, and you just couldn't find an all-round wholesomer farm than Uncle Sagamore's. We're going to stay on here, Pop says, and not even go back to the tracks at all, which suits me fine. Things are already beginning to hum, now that him and Uncle Sagamore are back. They're sort of looking around for some new kind of business to go into, seeing that the leather didn't turn out so well, and I expect the whole place will begin to get exciting again real soon.

That's the nice thing about a farm. You never know what'll happen next.

THE END